Dear Romance Reader,

Welcome to a world of breathtaking passion and never-ending romance.

Welcome to *Precious Gem Romances*.

It is our pleasure to present *Precious Gem Romances,* a wonderful new line of romance books by some of America's best-loved authors. Let these thrilling historical and contemporary romances sweep you away to far-off times and places in stories that will dazzle your senses and melt your heart.

Sparkling with joy, laughter, and love, each *Precious Gem Romance* glows with all the passion and excitement you expect from the very best in romance. Offered at a great affordable price, these books are an irresistible value—and an essential addition to your romance collection. Tender love stories you will want to read again and again, *Precious Gem Romances* are books you will treasure forever.

Look for fabulous new *Precious Gem Romances* each month—available only at Wal★Mart.

Kate Duffy
Editorial Director

JUST AFTER MIDNIGHT

LORI HANDELAND

Zebra Books
Kensington Publishing Corp.
http://www.zebrabooks.com

ZEBRA BOOKS are published by

Kensington Publishing Corp.
850 Third Avenue
New York, NY 10022

Copyright © 1999 by Lori Handeland

Zebra and the Z logo Reg. U.S. Pat. & TM Off.

First Printing: October, 1999
10 9 8 7 6 5 4 3 2 1

Printed in the United States of America

everything came back with a piercing suddenness, and a sob escaped from her throat.

Papa.

Concern flooded the man's features, and he reached out to take Megan's hand. The warmth of his flesh covering hers soothed, and she turned her palm upward, winding her fingers through his. The stranger gave her a smile of encouragement that fair dazzled her, squeezed her hand, then withdrew his to stand.

A vague sense of disappointment flooded her at the loss of his warmth. She shook her head in irritation. She needed to get a hold of herself and find out what had become of her father. "Where am I, Mr.—"

"Lieutenant Carson, miss. Alex Carson. Northwest Mounted Police."

That explained the uniform, Megan thought, as she took in the red jacket, black pants, and knee-high boots.

"You're upstairs in one of the rooms at The Celebration," he continued. "And you are?"

"Megan Daily." She struggled to a sitting position on the bed and extended her hand, feeling slightly silly for doing so when he had already held her hand in a more intimate manner.

Alex Carson's lips twitched as though he'd read her thoughts, and then he grasped her fingers, drawing them toward his lips in a gesture at once Old World manners and yet too familiar. The return of the tingling warmth from his touch dismayed her. Megan withdrew her hand before his lips could meet her skin. "Daily?" He frowned. "You're Brian's daughter?"

"Yes." The tears gathered in her eyes again. She had to make him understand that this was all some terrible mistake. Her father would never die and leave her. He might go away for any amount of time, but he always came back. He promised her just that every time he left her behind, and Papa would never lie.

"Papa," she whispered, turning her gaze toward the window. "You always come back."

"Miss?"

Megan looked up into his concerned face and swallowed the rising tide of sorrow. Drawing herself up, she resolved to get to the bottom of the story. "Where's his body?" The sound of her voice, calm and crisp, the way it should be, steadied her.

"There's a graveyard for the victims at Dyea."

"I want to see his grave."

"Certainly, miss. I'm sure that can be arranged now that the weather has improved. You can never be sure any time before June."

Megan nodded absently as she got up from the bed. Dizziness assailed her, but she gritted her teeth and fought the black dots swimming before her eyes. By force of will she made the unaccustomed weakness recede and moved to the window.

Dawson City was a town of contrasts. The main streets boasted wooden structures, some elaborate, others barely standing, but each one a business of some sort built to serve the thriving boomtown. Beyond them, on the higher ground above the city proper, waved a sea of tents that housed the new arrivals, greenhorns or *cheechakos* as they were called by the veteran sourdoughs. The street below Megan's window buzzed with activity. Men, women, mules, dogs—every living being strove to slog through the boggy mud Front Street had become that spring. Yet no mountain was too high to climb in search of gold—the illusive, the unobtainable.

Megan sighed and turned away. How well she knew the worship of the great god greed. She had been following her father in his daily devotions for the past ten of her twenty-six years. It looked as though this time Papa's god had eluded him forever.

"Are you feeling better now, Miss Daily?"

Though the words were quiet, Megan started nonetheless. Her gaze went to the handsome Mountie, and again she knew a tug of response when her eyes met his. Perhaps she should avoid this man and the strange sensations his presence engendered within her. But her need to see her father's grave ran deep, and so she nodded her head in assent.

Alex Carson's face and eyes lit with a smile, and Megan smiled in return, despite the heaviness within her heart.

"If you'd like, I can go now and arrange for you to return to the outside by way of Dyea."

The smile froze on Megan's face. "I beg your pardon?"

"You can see your father's grave on the way back to your home. Dyea is several hundred miles from here, but it's at the bottom of the pass if you plan to go that way. I'd be happy to take care of the arrangements for you."

"Why would I leave? This is my home now."

Alex frowned. "A lady like you has no place here. This is a dance hall."

He said the words as though there were a sour taste in his mouth, and Megan's brows drew together in confusion. "I know what The Celebration is, Lt. Carson. What I don't understand is the problem."

"Men pay women to dance with them." Alex spoke slowly, as though to a child. "Among other things, I'm sure."

"As far as I'm concerned, the women here fulfill a needed service in keeping lonely miners company. As my father explained things in his letters, whores are housed on Paradise Alley. The girls here do nothing but dance. They make far and away enough money doing that, there's no need to sell themselves for anything more."

"And that's as it should be, Lovey."

A new voice caused both the lieutenant and Megan to turn toward the open doorway. Megan gaped. The woman standing there was the largest she had ever seen, not to mention the most colorful. A violet silk dressing gown tied with a green sash encased her ample figure. Blonde hair of a color not found in nature was piled on her head, adding to a height that must already have been six feet. Her face was painted artfully but heavily, and her long, pointed nails were blood red. Megan estimated her age to be somewhere between ancient and dead.

"Who," Megan asked, "are you?"

"Lovey, I'm your best friend." The woman cackled at her own wit and entered the room.

Megan drew back as the woman bore down on her, enveloping Megan in the scent of violets. Megan's back met the wall with a thump, and the woman cackled again before placing one long, red fingernail beneath Megan's chin and turning her face from side to side in the sunlight.

"You've got possibilities, Lovey. Definite possibilities."

"What are you talking about, Queen?"

Alex's angry voice brought Megan back to her senses, and she jerked her face away from the brightly painted woman.

"Here now, there's no cause to get testy with old Queen Love. I want to help."

"She doesn't need your help. She's not staying."

Queen Love turned to Megan. "Is that the way of it, Lovey?"

"Ah . . . no." Megan shook her head to clear the foggy smell of violets and sunshine from her senses, then said more firmly, "No. I plan to manage The Celebration just as I did our restaurant in San Francisco. That was my father's plan all along."

"You mean you came here to take over this place?" Alex's voice was incredulous as he stared at Megan.

"Certainly."

"I never would have expected you for a whore."

Megan gasped. What had happened to the sweet gentleman who had helped her? When had he been replaced by this sneering bigot? She had been right all along. A man was a man, no question about it.

"Now, Lieutenant, the girls don't whore. The Celebration ain't no cigar store."

"And how many of the girls on Paradise Alley started out as dancers, Queen? You know as well as I do that there's a thin line between respectable and whore in the Yukon." He glared at Megan. "It's only a matter of time."

Megan stepped away from the wall and crossed the distance between herself and the Mountie. "You, sir—" She jabbed her finger into his red clad chest. "—can get out of my dance hall."

"Gladly." After a sharp nod that was both sneer and dismissal, Alex Carson left the room, his footsteps clattering down the wood stairs and retreating toward the front door.

"Good riddance," Megan muttered.

"Well now, Lovey, he's got his troubles, same's the rest of us. Don't judge him too harsh before you know his reasons."

"He can't possibly have a reason to explain that behavior." Megan stared at the door for a moment, an odd sense of loss flooding her at the Mountie's abrupt departure. Shrugging off the feeling as exhaustion from her trip, she turned to the other woman. "Tell me about my father."

The heavy makeup on Queen's face sagged

along with her expression. "I'm sorry you heard the way you did, Lovey. That dolt Zechariah shouldn't have blurted the news out to you thataway. He was told to come for me." She sighed. "Well, there's no help for it now. How're you feeling?"

"Like I stepped into a dream. I can't believe he's dead." Megan sank onto the edge of the bed.

Queen joined her and, as the mattress dipped alarmingly, Megan braced herself before she could be thrown against the woman's side.

"The sad news is true. Brian's gone to meet his maker. That's a meeting I would have paid good money to see." She cackled again before continuing. "I've been running the place since he died. Now that you're here, you can have the job. I'd much rather do my job and be done with it."

"And what is your job, Queen?" Megan found herself intensely curious about this giant of a woman.

"They come for miles to pay me a dollar a dance."

Megan's eyes widened. Men came for miles to dance with Queen Love? The prospect amazed her.

"I see what you're thinkin'. I don't understand it either, but men love me. Always have."

Megan had no idea how to respond, but Queen obviously did not need a response since she began to talk about the workings of The Celebration in a businesslike tone in direct contrast to her appearance. Megan's head swam with the unfamiliar details of dance hall ownership.

When her mother had died a few weeks after Megan's thirteenth birthday, her father left her to be raised by a maiden aunt in Chicago while he went off to seek his first fortune. Aunt Saundra owned a dry goods store, and Megan had first learned about business at the older woman's side. By the time Brian returned for a visit, three years later, Megan was running the store on her own and turning a larger profit than her aunt had ever dreamed possible. When her father saw the asset Megan would be to any of his ventures, he told her to pack up her meager collection of belongings, and they hit the road.

She spent the next ten years of her life managing restaurants and hotels in different boomtowns throughout the country. She had little time to lament her lost youth, though sometimes when she was alone in her bed, she dreamt of what her life might have been like if she'd remained with her aunt—dresses and dances, music and men. Instead of those sweet trappings of young womanhood, Megan witnessed the seamy side of male-female relationships. She had seen too many good women brought low for the love of an unworthy male. It was a hard lesson, but one Megan had seen played out too often to forget.

A half hour later, Queen paused for breath and Megan jumped in. "Queen, I think I should rest. This has all been too upsetting."

"Sure it has, Lovey. You lie down, and I'll come back to get you when the dance hall opens. You can just watch things tonight. Later we'll move you into your papa's rooms. You can stay there while you're here."

Megan frowned. "What do you mean 'while I'm here'?"

Queen shrugged. "Nothin'. I don't figure that you'll be stayin' overly long. This is a tough town, a hard life."

"I've lived my life in boomtowns for the past ten years. I may not look strong, but I am." Megan lifted her chin. "I'll be staying, Queen."

"You can sell out and make a tidy profit, go back to an easier life in San Francisco."

"I'm not a quitter. This dance hall is the only thing I have left of my father, and I don't plan to sell it to the highest bidder. I'm not going to disgrace his faith in me by turning tail and running when things get a little rough."

"Hmm . . ." Queen stared at her for a long moment, blood-red nail tapping equally bright lips. "Well, we'll see. You'll learn soon enough that Dawson City's not like the rest of the world. Get some rest now."

Megan gritted her teeth. She'd had to prove her worth in each and every town they'd done business in; why should Dawson City be any different?

After thanking Queen for her help, Megan closed the door and climbed back into bed. She tossed and turned for several moments before giving up. Reaching into the pocket of her dress, Megan withdrew a worn piece of paper.

June 1, 1897

Dearest Daughter,

I am sure the incredible news has reached you in San Francisco by now. Gold has been struck in the Klondike. Yes, gold, dear girl. Your papa's luck has come in at last. But Brian Daily is not so foolish as to break his back searching for the glittering dust. No, I have opened a saloon and dance hall for the hard-working miners. Their newfound wealth has made me a rich man.

Come immediately, Meggie, my girl. I need your help and "The Celebration" could use your organizational skills. Sell the eatery and use the funds for your trip. I instruct you to travel by water route to Dawson City as quickly as possible. Do not, under any circumstances, proceed by land. Dead Horse Trail awaits the unwary. Since the rivers freeze early in the land of the midnight sun, you must hurry to the Klondike with all speed. If all goes well, I hope to set eyes upon your lovely face before winter sets in.

Your papa

The paper swam before her eyes, then fell to the floor as Megan raised her hands to her face and wept.

As afternoon gave way to evening with no visible change in the brightness of the sun, Alex strode down the mud-soaked main street of Dawson City, angry with himself and Megan Daily. When she had literally fallen into his arms, his surprise had quickly given way to interest when his gaze took in the smooth perfection of her skin. She looked so young lying unconscious in his arms that he had felt an overwhelming urge to protect her. But when she awoke and told him who and what she was, his male regard had wavered on the edge of disgust. Still, there was something about her eyes that haunted him.

Alex shook his head. He didn't have time for a woman, especially that woman. He'd asked to be placed on the force in the Yukon because he had a purpose here. He needed to concentrate on that purpose.

Reaching his quarters in the barracks of the mounted police, Alex undressed and threw himself onto his bunk. He stared at the sun's reflection across the plank wall and remembered—Joanna. Pretty, innocent, trusting Joanna. Why had she run away from home? Who had killed her?

He had traced his sister to The Celebration and then to Paradise Alley. She had died a prostitute in a filthy, backwater street—his sweet Joanna. Rage filled him at the thought. He had been too late to save her; but he was not too late to make whoever had abandoned her in Dawson City pay for that mistake.

Unless, of course, that man had been Brian Daily. If his suspicions proved correct, the only revenge Alex would have would be the hope that Brian roasted in Hell throughout eternity.

TWO

Megan spent the remainder of her first afternoon in the Klondike berating herself over the death of her father. If she had only reached Dawson City before the ice set in, she would have been here to prevent his ill-fated trip to the outside. If she had come with Brian on this trip, rather than remaining behind, she could have stopped him. If, if, if . . . Her head ached from the tears and the guilt and the memories.

Hours later Megan sat up wearily. Glancing at the clock, she jumped to her feet. Queen would be along any minute to take her downstairs, and she wasn't even dressed yet. The way the blasted sun shone day and night, it was a wonder anyone knew the time.

Since her trunks were nowhere in sight, Megan used the cool water in a pitcher on the dresser to bathe her tear-sore eyes, resolving to change her travel dress when she located her clothes. Her hair had come loose sometime during the afternoon, and she deftly smoothed the long, red tresses into the severe bun she'd adopted long ago to offset her youth.

"Well, Lovey, I must say you do look worse for the wear."

Megan started. The woman had a knack for catching her unaware. Obviously Queen never entertained the notion of knocking before she entered a room.

"I need to change my dress, Queen. Do you know if my trunks have arrived from the ship?"

"Sure thing, Lovey. I had them put in your pa's room." The immense woman looked Megan up and down critically. "I hope you have somethin' in those trunks more presentable than that."

Her earth-toned traveling costume was the height of fashion in San Francisco, but she could see how the dress would be out of place in a dance hall. "I do have a few more-colorful dresses to wear when I'm working."

Queen sniffed. "Good thing, too. You look like a little, brown bird in that rag. We'd best hurry now if you want to get downstairs before the music starts." She turned and left the room quickly for a person of such girth.

Hurrying to keep pace with Queen, Megan nearly bumped into the woman when she stopped abruptly in front of a set of double doors a few yards down the long hallway. Opening the doors with a flourish, Queen stepped back and allowed Megan to enter ahead of her.

Taking several steps into the room, Megan looked around for her belongings, but stopped abruptly, her mouth falling open in amazement at the opulence of her father's suite.

Electric light reflected off the highly polished wood floor. Draperies of scarlet velvet obscured the windows. Dominating the chamber, a magnificent four-poster bed stood covered with a blanket of white fur. On the far side of the room, a Turkish bath was visible backed by a wall of mirrors. Megan found the decor of the suite masculine but for the fresh wildflowers that filled several vases. Their fragrance floated to her on the warm air. To her right, another set of double doors opened onto a sitting room, complete with a fireplace. Above the mantel, a large painting of a frail, flame-haired woman occupied the position of honor.

"Mama," Megan whispered in amazement.

"She was right beautiful, your mama," Queen said, her voice quiet for the first time since Megan had met her.

"I've never seen that painting before."

"Your pa had it painted right here in Dawson City once The Celebration began to make money. He must have loved her somethin' fierce."

"He did." Megan paused, staring transfixed at the image she had nearly forgotten. "I thought he'd go to pieces when she died. I was only thirteen."

"You were what kept him goin' through those tough times, I'm sure. He loved you. Talked about you nonstop." Queen made a shooing motion with her large, painted fingers. "You'd better get dressed. The curtain'll go up in fifteen minutes whether I'm on stage or not."

Megan nodded and crossed the room to her trunks beneath the window. Opening one, she pulled out the first dress she found and was pleased to see her favorite dark-lavender silk with the leg-of-mutton sleeves and godet skirt.

Glancing toward the door, she found Queen lounging against the wall, her gaze on Megan. The woman couldn't expect her to change while she watched, could she? Megan raised her eyebrows while nodding at the door. Queen hoisted her huge frame into a standing position. "All right, I'll go. But I can tell you, there ain't nothin' beneath that brown disgrace for a dress that I haven't seen before. Many times."

When the door closed behind Queen, Megan gave a sigh of relief as she murmured, "Maybe so, but I've never undressed in front of anyone in my life, and I don't plan to start with you."

Quickly removing her traveling costume, Megan slipped into the dress. The cool, smooth silk felt wonderful and the familiarity of the oft-worn fabric soothed her. She rubbed both hands up and down her shoulders, breathing deeply to calm herself. She could think of nothing she wanted to do less than face people with her heart bruised and battered. But her father would expect her to do her job, and that was what she would do.

When Megan opened the door, she found Queen leaning over the wood railing observing the dance hall below. "Got a full house for your first night." The woman turned and her mouth dropped open with surprise.

"What's the matter?" Megan asked, looking down to see if anything were amiss. Finding nothing unbuttoned or torn, she turned her bewildered gaze upon Queen.

"You're not going to wear that?" Queen's mouth curled in distaste.

"Of course. This is my favorite dress, and it's perfect since I'm in mourning."

"Mourning? You can't be serious."

"Of course I'm serious. My father is dead. Just because we're in the wilds of the Yukon doesn't mean I shouldn't show proper respect. Though I may have spent the last ten years working day and night for profit, my mother taught me what's right."

Queen bit her lip as though she didn't know what to say next. But she didn't remain silent for long. "Proper respect is one thing; business is another. Brian would understand what needs to be done to keep up appearances, and that ain't it." Queen came closer and lowered her voice as though to share a secret. "Lovey, you look like a spinster schoolteacher with that gown buttoned all the way to your chin and no skin a-showin' anywhere, not to mention the color. My dead aunt has clothes with more zip. And I wasn't goin' to say anything about your hair, but I guess I'd better. Why do you put such pretty red hair up in an old bun? Take advantage of youth, girl; it don't last forever."

"I'm not a dance-hall girl, Queen. I'm the *owner* of The Celebration."

"That don't make no difference. I know the men that come in here, and you'll make them squirm lookin' like their old Aunt Hattie. It'll ruin business; mark my words."

Megan frowned. The clothes she wore and the way she did her hair had never put off any of the customers in her other establishments. Sure, Brian had been around then to smooth over any rough spots between her and the men. He had always made his meaning clear—his daughter was off limits for courting; she was present merely as a manager. She just had to make the same rules understood at the outset.

"Queen, what I wear is of no consequence, I'm sure," Megan said in the no-nonsense tone of voice she'd found worked best with employees. "Let's get downstairs or you'll miss the first dance."

Queen shook her head and grumbled all the way down the wooden staircase. But the dancer kept any further opinions of Megan's appearance confined to muttered words beneath her breath.

The Celebration was geared up for a night of revelry, the dance hall full of men waiting for the show to begin. Queen abandoned Megan at the foot of the stairs and hurried to her place behind the curtain while Megan drifted toward the entryway between the dance hall and the middle room designated for gambling. That room was also full. A glance through to the front room, or saloon, revealed a crowd of men there, as well. Megan smiled—nothing better than a full house.

When she turned back to the dance hall, silence descended over the room at her back. Curious, she turned around only to see every man at every table staring in her direction. When they saw her looking, each one became busy with his cards. Feeling uneasy for the first time she could recall, Megan returned to the dance hall, but the pressure of countless eyes bored into her back as she left.

In the dance hall proper, the attention of the men remained focused on the stage, and Megan took a position near the back of the room to wait for the curtain to rise.

After a flourish from the musicians, the red-and-gold curtain moved upward and the feet, then legs, then bodies of the girls on stage became visible. The crowd hooted, hollered, and stamped their feet as, for the next several hours, they were entertained by the dancing girls.

Megan kept to the rear, observing the crowd and her employees. She was amazed at Queen's dancing ability and the responsiveness of the men to her talent. The woman hadn't been exaggerating her appeal to the opposite sex. When the show was over and the women began to mingle with the customers, men surrounded Queen, begging the boon of her first dance.

After a short intermission to wet dry throats, the dancing began. For one dollar a song, a lonely miner could dance with the girl of his choice; and for every dollar spent at the bar, the girl received a circular disc to represent her share of the profits. An energetic dancer with a persuasive attitude could make her fortune in the Klondike.

Megan made her way to the end of the polished wood bar and watched the bartenders serve drinks. A small scale was available so gold dust could be weighed for payment, and she was impressed with the speed and accuracy of the bartenders' measurements. After she had been observing for nearly half an hour, the room began to empty.

"Why is everyone leaving so early?" Megan asked one of the bartenders. "I thought the dance halls were full until morning."

He cleared his throat, swallowed. "Well, miss, I don't know how to say this." He reddened before continuing in a rush of words. "You make the men uncomfortable. They're used to seein' the girls here. They don't know what to make of you."

Megan turned to look at her reflection in the wall of mirrors behind the bar. Nothing was amiss. Maybe she was a bit pale, but that was to be expected after the long journey and the horrible news that had awaited her upon arrival.

"The men come in here to blow off steam," he continued. "They drink and dance. Have a good time. They don't like to be reminded of their wives and mothers by lookin' at you."

Megan sighed. Had Queen been right? Was she bad for business? But what could she do? She didn't know how to be anyone but herself.

She nodded to the bartender and retreated to the dance hall. As the night wore on, a steady stream of men exited The Celebration. Toward morning, Queen made her way to where Megan sat in a darkened corner of the dance hall. Seating her ample bulk on the remaining chair, Queen leaned back and kicked off her shoes. "Hate to say I told you so, Lovey."

Megan straightened, suddenly angry. No one had a right to pass judgment on the way she looked. What difference could her appearance possibly make to her ability to manage The Celebration?

"I don't know what you're talking about, Queen. People are tired tonight, that's all. Tomorrow will be better, I'm sure."

At Queen's doubtful expression, Megan suddenly stood up. "I want to meet the rest of the girls. Come on." She strode across the room toward the stage where the other dancers sat perched on the structure's edge, their stocking feet swinging above the neat row of shoes below.

At Megan's approach, the other women's attention focused on her. She saw varying degrees of distrust and dislike on each of their faces. This was not going to be easy.

Queen joined her and introduced each of the colorfully adorned women. Their names were a kaleidoscope of sound: Blue Mary, Sassy Sue, the Lightning Bolt, Gilded Lily, and many others. It seemed that everyone had an alias in Dawson City. The more unusual the name, the better. Would she ever be able to place each face with the odd monikers to which they belonged?

"As you've probably heard, I'm Megan Daily, Brian's daughter. I'll be running the place from now on. I hope we can all work together to make The Celebration a success." Her smile felt stiff, but she used it anyway, hoping to establish a rapport.

A tall, painfully thin woman jumped down from the stage. "If you'd stop driving off the men with your old-maid's ways, we might have a chance."

"Ah . . . Skinny . . . um . . . Nell," Megan stuttered, unfamiliar with the strange form of address. "I'm sure that in a few days the men will get used to me and business will go on as usual." Megan glanced at the other women. Skepticism shrouded every face.

"We'll see, Miss Daily." Skinny Nell stared into Megan's eyes, taking her measure, before continuing. "If'n things don't improve by next week, we'll all have to go somewhere's else to do our dancin'."

Nods of agreement from the others had Megan opening her mouth to argue the point, but a commotion from the front bar drew her attention.

"Aw, hell," groaned Queen, putting her hand to her forehead.

"What is it?" Megan demanded.

"Thought he'd be gone for a while yet. I didn't want to have to burden you with more bad news after you learned about your pa."

"Who are you talking about? What bad news?"

"Big Ian McMurphy's who, and he's enough bad news for the entire Yukon." Queen nodded toward the entrance to the dance hall.

Megan followed the woman's gaze and her heart

leapt to her throat. The man wasn't addressed as "big" just for conversation. He filled the doorway, ducking his head to enter. Mammoth shoulders strained at a coat of silver fur while legs the size of unsplit logs pushed at the seams of his black pants. McMurphy's black beard, shot through with silver that matched the fur, obscured the lower half of his face; but his bright, black eyes shone with a feral intelligence. Their light turned to Megan and she gulped.

"Owns nearly everything in the territory," Queen whispered, "and he's got his eye on this place since Brian died. He doesn't look too happy to see you." For once Queen's voice was unamused, her high-pitched cackle glaringly absent.

There was no time to say anything more as McMurphy stopped in front of her. The girls shuffled away, but Queen remained at her side. Megan spared a grateful glance for the woman, but Queen's wary gaze was focused on the huge man. Megan quickly returned her attention to the threat of Ian McMurphy. She tilted her neck back, then back even further, to look up into his face.

"Heard you came to town, little girl." The giant's voice boomed, causing Megan to flinch. The room had gone silent, the few patrons who remained moving closer to observe the confrontation.

Megan drew herself up to her full height of five feet eight inches, though no doubt she looked like a dwarf next to Queen and McMurphy. "How can

I help you, sir?" She made her voice as cold as she'd heard the Yukon was in December.

Big Ian McMurphy was not impressed. In fact, Megan thought she saw the shadow of a smile play around his lips before he spoke. "Well, missy, had my eye on this place for a long time now. I don't have a dance hall and I've decided I want one. Your father wasn't much, but he knew how to start a business."

Megan bristled at the insult to her father but attempted to keep the confrontation civil. "The Celebration isn't for sale, Mr. McMurphy. I am perfectly capable of taking care of the place myself."

Ian glanced at her clenched fists, and this time the smile he turned upon her was genuine. "So, you're a fighter. That's good. I haven't had to fight for what I wanted in a long, long time. This should be interesting."

"Leave the child alone," Queen said. "Go pick on someone your own size."

"Like you?" His face softened and he laughed, the sound something between a chuckle and a growl. "I'd be delighted."

McMurphy made a move toward Queen; but before he could complete his intent, a voice from the doorway halted him in midstride. "McMurphy, you've been warned to stay out of trouble."

Megan looked up and a shiver of awareness ran down her spine as she met the angry blue eyes of Alex Carson.

"Carson, why is it you always show up where you're not wanted?" McMurphy swung his im-

mense body across the room and jammed his face
close to the Mountie's. "I'm getting a mite tired
of you pesterin' me."

With admirable calm, the lieutenant stepped forward and jabbed his forefinger against the man's
massive chest. "Pestering is my job. Especially when
it involves bullies who delight in snatching others'
hard-earned property. What are you doing here,
McMurphy? This place belongs to Miss Daily now."

The lieutenant never glanced at Megan, and her
name came off his lips sounding as if he found
the taste of the words sour. Nevertheless, she was
impressed with the way he handled the mountain-
ous man, standing up to him without blinking. Ian
McMurphy scared her witless, though her years of
dealing with rough men had schooled her not to
show any fear in their presence.

After several seconds of tense silence, McMurphy
turned and bowed stiffly to Megan and Queen.
"Ladies, it's been a pleasure. I'll be back when
things are less stifling." McMurphy brushed past
Alex without a glance, and the crowd parted in a
backward rush as he marched to the door.

"He's a nasty one." Alex had moved so close his
breath brushed Megan's neck and she started.
"You should stay clear of him."

Megan trembled at the sensation and turned to
look into the lieutenant's eyes. For a moment she
glimpsed something akin to concern in the blue
depths before they became shuttered and cold
once again.

"If you're smart, you'll sell your time to anyone but Big Ian."

Megan scowled at the insult and her anger rose. If he wanted to believe the worst of her, she wouldn't disappoint him. Smiling coyly as she'd observed other women do when they dealt with men, Megan ran her fingertip down the side of Alex Carson's face. "I have no need to sell my time. But if I did, perhaps you'd be interested, Lieutenant Carson."

Her finger tingled from the warmth of his face and the stubble shading his jaw. Their eyes met and suddenly she no longer felt like teasing the man. Something hot and dangerous had come to life in his eyes, and Megan stepped back, jerking her finger away from his face.

Alex continued to stare at her for a moment. Then he turned on his shiny-booted heel and left The Celebration without another word.

"I don't think you should tease the poor boy, Lovey. Unless, of course, you're interested in what your teasing might give rise to." Queen cackled and slapped Megan on the back so hard she stumbled foreword. The woman caught her arm. "Sorry. I forget my own strength sometimes, and you're such a skinny, little thing. You know that lieutenant's got a reputation around here for being a cool one, hard as ice in January, too. Those blue eyes, though, they're like to give me the shivers."

Megan didn't answer, just continued to stare out the door through which Alex Carson had disappeared. What an infuriating, confusing man.

She was not used to confusion. Especially where men were concerned. The life she'd lived had given her a knowledge of men's ways. They might come in all shapes, colors, and sizes, but a man was a man was a man. Smart women steered clear of the entire species. The only man she had ever had the slightest use for was her father, and he had been as dependable as a gold mine.

Thoughts of her father brought tears to her eyes, and Megan swallowed over a thick knot in her throat. Without saying good night to anyone, she turned and fled up the stairs.

Slamming the door of her room behind her, Megan leaned against the heavy oak. How was she ever going to go on without her father? He hadn't been dependable, but she'd always known there was someone in the world who needed her, who loved her. She had made herself into the kind of daughter he would always need at his side, but she had never considered he might die and leave her alone forever. The desolation and fear she had felt as a thirteen-year-old girl, left with a woman she barely knew as she watched her last surviving parent walk away from her, rose up in a wave of sadness. With determination born through years of practice, she pushed away the pain and the loneliness, vowing to pour all her love into the business her father had left in her care.

THREE

Megan stood at the back door of The Celebration and cast her gaze over the dance hall. One week after her arrival . . . and the place became emptier every night. The girls' glares had graduated from annoyed to hostile. She would be out several dancers if business didn't improve soon; then Ian McMurphy would be able to take The Celebration without any fight, and she would be out on the street with nowhere to go in the world. If she weren't careful, she could end up selling herself to stay alive. Then all of Alex Carson's dire predictions would come true.

Megan opened the back door and stepped into the heat and sunshine of a Yukon evening in July. She found it hard to believe summer temperatures could reach 120 degrees when 70 degrees below zero was common during the nine-month winter. She lifted her face to the sun, leaned against the side of the building and closed her eyes. Just when she was beginning to relax, something cold and wet pushed against her hand, startling her. Megan's eyes flicked open and she glanced down. The scream stuck in her throat.

Standing at her feet was the largest wolf she had ever seen—pure black and sleek, his head tilted to the side as he studied her. Megan held her breath while the huge animal leaned over to sniff her skirt. Seeming to recognize her, he wagged his tail and again pushed his nose into her hand. After a moment's hesitation, Megan tentatively patted the animal's large head. The wolf rubbed against her good-naturedly.

"I wonder where you came from, boy?"

As if in answer, the wolf's hackles rose and a low rumble issued from his throat. Megan jumped, yanked her hand out of harm's way as her heart thumped hard and fast. The animal had seemed so friendly. Then she saw he stared past her and toward the door.

"What're you doin' out here, Lovey? The show's about to start." As usual, the volume of Queen's voice would have startled the dead. Her eyes went to the wolf and she gasped. "Damon! Where did he come from?"

"You know him?"

"I should say I do. That's your father's wolf—part dog, too, he thought. Brian took the animal with him wherever he went, and we all thought it was killed with Brian in the avalanche. Guess we were wrong." Queen eyed the animal warily. "Too damned bad."

"Don't you like him?" The wolf now stood pressed against Megan's knee, though he continued to grumble whenever Queen spoke. "He seems harmless enough."

"Damon never could abide anyone but Brian. Your pa found him by the river and raised him up from a little tyke. He seems to have taken to you though. Maybe he knows you're Brian's kin. I don't know as I'd trust him though."

Damon shifted and growled. Megan glanced down to find the animal now glared at Queen, hackles still up. Ignoring Queen's advice, she patted the mammoth head. At the touch of her hand, Damon relaxed and sat, staring up at her with openmouthed devotion.

"Maybe so, but what am I supposed to do with him?"

"That's up to you. Right now I've got to get back to work. You comin'?"

After another glance at the wolf, Megan nodded and followed Queen inside. When she turned to shut the door, she saw that Damon was at her heels. "No, boy. You have to stay outside." She knelt so she was at eye level with the animal. "Listen, if you stay here and behave, I'll bring dinner later."

The animal cocked its head, his odd yellow eyes seeming to bore into hers. Then he trotted out and curled up against the wall, tucking his nose beneath his tail. Megan gave a sigh of relief and closed the door. Since the wolf had belonged to her father, she would have to do something with the creature.

She followed Queen inside and stood with her

at the rear of the dance hall. The sight of only a half-dozen men waiting for the show made Megan's heart sink. She had been so hoping the crowds would improve as the miners became used to her.

"Another bad night," Queen observed.

"I don't want to hear about it, Queen. I just don't." Megan rubbed at the headache beginning between her eyes.

Hours later, the headache was no longer just beginning but had become a living, breathing entity in Megan's brain. She sat at her usual table near the back and watched the unoccupied dancers glare at her.

"Well, missy, looks like business is really booming for you."

Megan's head thumped at the volume of Ian McMurphy's voice next to her ear and she groaned. "What do you want, McMurphy?"

She was in no mood to be civil to anyone, least of all him. She might have been afraid of him on his last visit; now she was merely irritated. The impending loss of her dance hall made fear of anyone or anything seem irrelevant.

"Just thought I'd stop by and see if the rumors were true. At the rate your business is going out the door, you'll have to pay me to take this place off your hands." He laughed.

"You worry about your business and I'll take care of mine."

"You're doing a great job so far."

"Get out," she said, though she didn't bother to look at him.

He grabbed her by the arms and yanked her to her feet. "Look at me when we're talking business."

Though her feet now dangled above the floor, Megan looked into McMurphy's angry eyes. "Put me down. Then get out."

He let her go and she dropped to the floor; but before she could step out of his way, he placed a huge paw upon her shoulder. "I'll leave when I'm good and ready, missy."

"My name's not *missy*," Megan snapped as she managed with no little difficulty to extricate herself from his clutches.

A black flash at the edge of her vision caused Megan to turn quickly, just in time to see Damon lunge for Ian's throat. McMurphy was quick for his size and managed to ward off the animal with a swipe of his ham-like forearm. The dog fell to the floor, then rolled up and into a crouch, growling, teeth bared, as he prepared to leap again.

"Damon, no," Megan shouted. The animal backed down, but the hair on his neck remained at attention as he trotted over to sit near her feet. He continued to emit low rumbles as he glared at McMurphy.

Megan looked up to meet the speechless gapes of Ian and the small group of employees who had gathered around.

"Only Brian could control him like that," Queen said.

Megan swallowed the lump in her throat. "Now,

I can." She was surprised to find her headache had disappeared.

"Well, Mr. McMurphy, I suggest you leave my dance hall before I let Damon finish what he began."

Ian warily eyed the dog as he backed toward the door. "I'll be back when you're out of business, Miss Daily. I'm sure you'll be glad to see me then."

As soon as McMurphy was out of sight, Megan collapsed into a chair. She patted Damon's head and the dog stared at her with adoration.

"Who let him in?"

"Me," Zechariah called from behind the bar "McMurphy's got quite a temper and it looked like you meant to rile him, so I let Damon on in. He must have decided you're to be protected."

"Lucky for me," Megan said as she remembered what it felt like to be held captive in McMurphy's huge hands.

"What did Ian say to you?" At the sound of Queen's voice, Damon flattened his ears against his head and he snarled. Queen backed up a few steps, but the dog retreated at a snap of Megan's fingers.

Megan ignored Queen's question, answering instead the question that had haunted her own mind. "I'm not going to let that man have the only gift my father ever gave me. Not without a fight. You said a few changes in my appearance would help with the business."

"Well—" Queen looked her up and down doubtfully. "—I didn't say just a few."

Megan waved her hand at Queen's skepticism.

Now that she'd decided upon this, nothing would stop her from going forward. "Whatever it takes. Since we're required to close at midnight to observe the Lord's day, do you think you can have me ready by show time Monday?"

"I can sure try. But you know it's more than how you dress that needs changin'; there's your attitude, too. There's ways of lookin' at a man, promisin' without actually followin' through." She peered at Megan. "Still, I think with a little practice, we might just bring you up to snuff, Lovey. You've got the looks; that helps." With a sigh she turned to the other dancers. "Come on, girls; we've got work to do."

Megan snapped her fingers for Damon and followed Queen and the girls upstairs.

The evening of July third arrived, sunny and hot. Not unusual for July, except that in Dawson City the sun would continue to shine throughout the night. Since the majority of the population in Dawson City was American, not Canadian, the approaching holiday had brought everyone in the surrounding areas to town. As a result, the saloons and dance halls on Front Street were filled with miners and townsfolk. The Celebration was not excluded from the crush of people eager to commemorate the spirit of American independence. For the first time in a week, the dance hall was packed with men waiting for the show to begin.

Upstairs, Megan contemplated her reflection in the mirrored wall behind the bath, and her heart moved into her throat. What was she doing? The woman staring back at her bore no resemblance to the Megan Daily she knew so well. This woman was indeed Meggie O'Day, the name Queen had insisted she adopt with her new appearance.

"Megan is much too stiff," Queen had told her earlier as she brushed Megan's waist length hair. "To improve business you have to make the men feel comfortable with you. If you listen to me, Meggie O'Day can be the toast of this bog they call a town."

"I hate to pretend I'm someone else," Megan insisted.

"Lovey, how can you be someone else? That's silly. It's good business to present the merchandise to its best advantage."

"I'm not merchandise," Megan mumbled.

"I know you're not, but *they* don't know. Remember what I told you about men? They only believe what their eyes tell them is true. Keep 'em guessing, and we'll be the most successful dance hall this side of the Yukon River."

Megan had relented in the end, and now she stood waiting to descend the stairs, mount the stage, and introduce the girls for their late-night show. Queen thought she should make an entrance and allow her new appearance to stir up the crowd. Megan wasn't so sure, but she had decided to let Queen have her way in this.

The musicians began to play a lively tune and Megan gave her hair one last, unneeded, pat. The time had come to show herself to the world.

FOUR

All night Alex had been drawn toward The Celebration as he made his rounds through the streets of Dawson City. As the clock neared midnight, he gave in to the urge and entered the dance hall, searching the crowd for Megan. He found it odd she wasn't somewhere downstairs with such a large mob present. Perhaps she was ill. For reasons he didn't care to examine, the thought nagged at him. He searched the rooms more thoroughly for a sign of her, pushing men aside so he could get a glimpse of those seated at the gambling tables and checking every bar to see if she might be working behind it. Just when he had decided to go upstairs and knock on the door to Brian's old rooms, music filled the dance hall and the crowd turned toward the stairway.

Alex walked farther into the packed room and followed the gaze of the crowd upward. His mouth fell open and he stopped abruptly to stare at the vision descending the staircase.

A dress of white satin clung suggestively to her form, the neckline too low, exposing most of her creamy breasts for inspection. A necklace of cut glass blinked brilliantly around her slim neck. Piled atop her head, her red hair sparkled with the stones glittering throughout the silky mass. A single, looped curl fell to her shoulder, drawing all eyes to the white satin of her throat. She rested a hand gloved in white on the head of the massive black wolf at her side. He, too, wore a collar of sparkling light.

Alex exhaled slowly, unable to believe this woman was the passably pretty Megan Daily dressed like a three-hundred-dollar whore for the entire Yukon to see. *What the hell was she playing at?*

Megan descended the rest of the stairs and made her way toward the front of the room. A small, shy smile played about her lips but she carried herself proudly through the crowd. Several of the men reached out to touch her, but a low rumble from the wolf at her side had them snatching their hands quickly away.

Megan gracefully ascended the stairs to the stage and positioned herself in the center of the floor. She raised her hand and, instantly, silence blanketed the room.

"Welcome to The Celebration, gentlemen." Her voice, low pitched and somewhat hoarse, had never sounded so seductive during the few conversations Alex had enjoyed with her. He frowned as the crowd went wild.

Megan flinched at the roar from the men. After swallowing deeply, she again smiled and lifted her hand. After a few moments the room quieted and she resumed speaking.

"I'm Meggie O'Day and you'll be seeing a lot of me from now on." She paused until the whoops and whistles died away. "Now, I give you the dancing girls of The Celebration." As the girls danced onto the stage, Megan scurried behind the curtain.

Alex clenched his teeth, staring at the curtain where Megan had disappeared. For just a moment when she'd stood on the stage, an image of Joanna had replaced Megan, his sister the object of hooting, drooling men, and the thought sent a sheet of hot, red rage throughout his body, warring with his guilt. Breathing deeply, Alex attempted to bring his emotions back under control. Joanna was dead, he reminded himself, and nothing he could do now would save her—but he could save Megan.

Determined to find out, Alex strode toward the stage. Ignoring the steps, he leapt onto the structure and walked into the wings.

Megan stood alone, deep in thought. When Alex grabbed her shoulder and spun her around to face him, she gasped. The wolf snarled, crouching low to spring, and Alex froze.

"Don't move," Megan said softly.

"I don't plan to." Alex held his breath. "Do something."

"Down, Damon. He won't hurt me," she reassured the wolf. "It's all right."

Damon continued to snarl, then began to circle Alex, his legs stiff and hackles raised.

"You'd better be more convincing. I don't think he believes you."

"Take your hand off me. Very slowly," Megan whispered.

Alex complied and the wolf eventually ceased snarling. Another sharp rebuke from Megan brought the animal back to her side, where he sat compliantly, though his feral eyes remained fixed on Alex's face. She patted the massive head and turned to Alex.

"You don't need to reward the beast for nearly tearing me apart," he said, irritated with her and her companion.

"Damon only wants to protect me. You'd do well to keep your hands to yourself like the rest of the men around here."

Alex clenched his fists with frustration, knowing any false moves could anger the wolf again. "What are you up to with this costume?"

"What costume?"

"Come on, Miss Daily, you certainly don't resemble the woman who fainted in my arms the day she arrived. Which is the act, the straightlaced woman of business or the high-priced whore?"

Megan's lips thinned. "As you've been told before, Lieutenant, The Celebration is not a brothel. The girls here can be bought for a dance—and a dance only. They have no need to sell themselves for anything more when they make so much merely by dancing."

"But you're not one of the girls, are you?"

"No, I'm not."

"Then what are you?"

"I'm the owner of this establishment, as I've told you several times. I'm beginning to think you're hard of hearing."

"No manager I've ever seen dressed like that."

"I've been persuaded that in the Yukon an owner does whatever is necessary to save her place. This—" She motioned to herself and shrugged "—has become necessary."

Alex stared into Megan's smoky-green eyes and saw the sadness beneath the anger. He sighed. "I'm sorry you've found it necessary to sell yourself."

"I'm not for sale, Lieutenant Carson."

"What would you call changing your appearance and your name to satisfy the men's distorted views and relieve them of their money?"

Megan tilted her chin up and looked him directly in the eye. "Survival."

The word caused him a momentary twinge of conscience. Perhaps she was right. He had no idea what it was like to be a woman alone. But he was beginning to get a picture.

"I don't mean to upset you," he said gently.

She tilted her head "You have."

"I've seen too many women drawn into a life of squalor. They all started out like you: pretty, young, in need of money. The combination is deadly."

Megan gave a tentative smile. "I appreciate your concern. Truly. But I own this place. All I'm trying to do is improve the business. If changing my appearance can help, I'm willing to be uncomfortable for a few hours."

"If you dress like one of the girls, the men will treat you like one of the girls. What do you plan to do about that?"

"I have Damon for protection. As you've seen for yourself, he doesn't approve of anyone touching me. The men will learn that I'm just for show and leave me alone."

Alex stepped toward her, surprised to find he had raised a hand to her face. "I doubt if any man could leave you alone, Megan." He cupped her defiantly raised chin in his palm.

She was so lovely—and she smelled so fresh, as though she had just stepped from a steaming bath filled with lemon-scented water. He breathed deeply of her fragrance as he rubbed weather-roughened knuckles along her cheek. Megan's eyes widened, but she didn't move away. Alex found himself wishing her into a dark, high-necked dress, the fire in her hair subdued by a schoolteacher's bun. Imagination was always better than revelation, he had found. Her mouth parted as though she expected him to kiss her.

What the hell? he thought, and lowered his head.

Boom. The volume of the sound shook the building, and they jumped away from each other. The wolf barked, then began to howl as the thunderous vibrations continued. Alex grabbed Megan's hand, and together they ran toward the front door of the dance hall in the wake of the crowd.

People filled the streets, cheering, dancing, and waving American flags. The Fourth of July had arrived. Every few minutes another cannon blast rent the air, and the noise of the crowd increased as their excitement mounted.

"What on earth is that horrible sound?" Megan put her hands to her ears.

"Blasting powder most likely. If you put the powder between two anvils and then run a red-hot iron between them—" He paused as another boom resounded from the end of the street. "—That's the sound you get."

A long, mournful howl ruptured the momentary stillness, and Alex looked toward The Celebration. Damon sat in the doorway, his nose turned up to the sky.

"Damon, go upstairs and be quiet." Megan waved her hand at the animal. "Go on, *now.*"

The black beast cocked its head at Alex, then narrowed its eyes as though wondering if the human were trustworthy. When another blast resounded, he started, then pulled his lips back in a snarl of warning before trotting back into the building.

Megan sighed. "Will this go on all night?"

"Probably. Then tomorrow there'll be a picnic with footraces and other track events. Should be quite a day."

"Races? Well, that should make people thirsty, especially if this heat keeps up."

"Do you ever think about anything but money?"

"What else is there?" Megan's glare dared him to contradict her.

"There's dogs swimming the river!" someone shouted as the crowd streamed toward the water.

"Damn," Alex swore. "I'd best get down there and find out what the trouble is."

"I'm going with you," Megan shouted above the crowd's roar and the blasting powder's thunder.

Alex paused to argue, then shrugged and set off toward the docks. He didn't have time to debate the issue with her. If she wanted to slog through the mud in her white satin, that was her choice.

He grabbed her wrist. "Stay near me. Since you sent your wolf home, these men might decide to do some touching while the touching's good."

She hesitated at his words, but a cheer from the crowd ahead had him hurrying away and Megan had no choice but to follow as he dragged her along.

He pushed his way to the front of the mass of people at the river's edge and was shocked at the sight that met his eyes. Hundreds of dogs swam frantically for the opposite bank.

"What's wrong with them?" Megan asked.

"The noise frightened 'em and they took off for the water," one of the miners answered. When the man turned to see who had asked the question, his eyes nearly popped from his head. "Meggie O'Day! Praise be, girl, ain't you a picture!"

Alex grimaced but said nothing. Since attention was what Megan wanted in that costume, she could deal with any results on her own, as long as the men didn't get too forward. He watched as she smiled and spoke with the man softly. She laughed and the sound sent shivers down Alex's spine.

Resolutely, he turned back to the river, then attempted to disperse the crowd.

When he looked for Megan a few moments later, she was nowhere to be seen. A shard of panic shot through his chest when he thought of her in the hands of the rough miners. He should have tied her to him.

A young shopkeeper noticed Alex's searching gaze. "If you're looking for Meggie, Lieutenant, she's down there." He pointed to the waterfront.

Alex spun around and saw her, up to her knees in the river, the white satin dress floating about. White gloves black with mud, she reached for a small, yellow puppy unable to keep its head above water for more than a few seconds at a time. The current kept pulling him under just as Megan's fingers brushed his head. Then the pup would bob to the surface a few feet away. Megan moved deeper and deeper into the river after the floundering dog. As Alex watched, she stretched out her hand, inching closer to the animal. The pup turned, paddling frantically toward her. Just as Megan bent to scoop the sopping dog into her arms, she lurched and fell beneath the water.

Alex sprang into the churning river, staring at the empty space where Megan had been seconds before. His heart beat faster as the time dragged on and there was no sign of her. Just when he was about to dive under the water, her head broke the surface and she floundered, obviously hampered by her skirts. As she went under again, he dove forward and his hand latched onto her arm. He pulled her upright and dragged her toward safety.

"No," she cried, coughing and sputtering on the muddy water she had swallowed. "I've got to get the puppy." She fought against him, her loose, wet hair whipping him in the face with the force of her struggles.

"Are you crazy? You nearly drowned." Alex wrapped his arms around her struggling form and continued toward solid ground. As soon as his feet touched bottom he stood and released her. Immediately Megan's gaze scanned the river.

"There." She pointed. "He's still alive."

She started into the water again, but Alex dragged her back. Her eyes clashed with his and he sighed. "Just stay here. I'll get the mutt."

He strode back into the river before she could argue. Within seconds he plucked the water-logged pup from the fray by the scruff of his neck. As he waded back toward Megan, the animal fell asleep against his chest, for all the world like a tired baby in its father's arms.

"Here." He thrust the animal into Megan's waiting hands.

"Thank you," she whispered, her face alight with gratitude. Suddenly her eyes focused on something past his shoulder and she frowned. "Look."

Alex followed her gaze, his eyes widening in amazement as he peered across the water.

The dogs had reached the far side and ran up and down the riverbank, yelping and howling at the crowd. Dogs tumbled over each other in their eagerness to get away from the continued thunder of the blasting powder. He had never seen so many animals in one place at the same time. Megan's wolf was probably the only canine left in the whole of Dawson City.

After a few more moments of laughing revelry, the crowd's interest waned and Alex was able to direct them back to town. There were still several hours left to drink, gamble, and dance before the fun began in earnest.

When Alex returned to where he'd left Megan, he let out a hiss of anger. At least a dozen miners, young and old, clustered around, talking to her and petting the sleeping pup. No one seemed to notice that Meggie O'Day's elaborate hairstyle now lay in wet snarls against her neck or that her stunning white dress was sodden with river water and streaked with mud. As for Megan, instead of being frightened by the men's rough attention, as any young lady should be, she seemed to glow and sparkle with vivacity. For some reason Alex found himself immensely annoyed with her happiness.

Pushing through the group of men, Alex took the dog from her and put the animal under his arm. Ignoring the pup's yelp of protest, he grabbed Megan by her soggy, satin-covered arm. "Let's go," he said and yanked her unceremoniously away from the others.

"Hold on," Megan shouted, pulling herself from his grasp. "These men were making me a business proposition."

Alex raised his eyebrows at her words. "Oh, really?"

"Not that kind of proposition." Megan gave him a look of pure exasperation. "Honestly. Would you watch how you're handling that poor dog?" She scowled at him before continuing. "They want me to have dinner and spend the day with the winner of the footrace at tomorrow's festivities. I think the public attention would be good for The Celebration." She turned back to the crowd of men. "Gentlemen, I accept your offer. I'll be there tomorrow morning."

"Wear somethin' flashy, Meggie. Give the winner a real treat," one of the older miners said as he leered toothlessly.

Megan looked uncomfortable for a moment, then she smiled and waved at the ancient lech before retreating quickly toward Alex. She attempted to retrieve the pup, but Alex shook his head and held on to the animal.

He took her arm again and strode toward The Celebration, his long gait causing Megan to hurry to keep up with him. He realized he was nearly dragging her through the mud, but he didn't care. When they reached the front of the dance hall, Alex released her. Her dress had fared well despite immersion in the river, though the satin slippers and gloves were surely ruined. Her hair hung in tangles around her face. Somehow, he liked it better that way. Alex glanced into the building and saw the crowd had increased with the news of her transformation.

"Your appearance seems to have brought in the business you were looking for, as well as other offers. Congratulations."

Megan didn't look inside, keeping her gaze on his face. "I do what I have to do. I thought you were beginning to understand that."

"I didn't think managing a dance hall would involve putting yourself up as a prize for the entire town to covet."

"Meggie O'Day represents The Celebration. The more interest there is in me, the more business for my dance hall. Can't you see this is all just good commerce?"

"I sure can, *Meggie*. You're every customer's dream." With his free hand, Alex tipped his hat with a flourish. "But I'm not buying."

Turning on his heel, he left Meggie O'Day standing in the muddy bog of Front Street without a backward glance. It wasn't until he reached his barracks that he realized he still held the sopping pup. A few moments later he knocked on the door of a friend's house to make a gift of the sleeping dog.

FIVE

Music. Voices. Laughter. The sounds increased in volume until Alex pulled a pillow over his head in an attempt to continue his disrupted slumber. It wasn't long before he realized the futility in his actions and threw the pillow against the wall with a frustrated growl. The Americans had been nothing but a nuisance to his English ancestors in 1776, why should they be anything different for him in 1898?

Alex's father was the youngest son of a titled English family. He had come to Canada looking for advancement in the service of his country. In the wild, untamed land he found his home as well as a French wife. Several years later, after the birth of four sons and one daughter, he received a letter from his family asking him to return to England. He declined, remaining to become a ranking officer in the Northwest Mounted Police. From the day of his birth, Alex, the eldest, was expected to follow in his father's wake. So far, he was well on his way to success.

The force in the Yukon was a team handpicked

from the best of the Northwest Mounted Police, itself an exclusive unit. When gold had been discovered on what was then Rabbit Creek, the Canadian government had sent the mounted police to Dawson City to keep order. They did not plan to let one of their properties succumb to the fate of American-held Scagway, Alaska, which had deteriorated into lawlessness with the advent of gold fever. Alex had been first in line to join the officers journeying to the Yukon, the opportunity for career advancement miraculously linked with his desires for truth and vengeance.

Alex was glad he had been assigned to patrol the festivities. If there was one thing the people in Dawson City knew how to do, it was celebrate, and he didn't want to waste a moment of the rare chance he had to mix work with pleasure. In a country where darkness reigned for most of the year, the opportunity to make merry in the sunshine would be used to utmost advantage. The scalding air tingled with anticipation, and Alex's own spirits rose higher than they had been since he arrived in the Yukon. He resolved to put memories of his sister and his thirst for revenge aside for the day and savor the Americans' frivolity.

A crowd had gathered in front of The Celebration and Alex frowned, memories of the previous night assaulting his peaceful frame of mind. Glancing over the heads of the men in front of him, Alex saw Megan displayed in the center of the porch. She was lovely, fresh, and bright in a dress the color of springtime leaves. The neckline scooped low, but at least her breasts were covered more adequately than they had been the last time he had seen her. She had pinned her hair into a loose roll at the back of her head with soft tendrils framing her face. A yellow straw hat, complete with white lace and roses, perched upon her head. Cheeks flushed to a pale peach from the heat and green eyes sparkling with excitement made an exquisite picture complete.

"Gentlemen!" A voice broke into Alex's reverie. "Line up and pay your entry fee. The winner of this race wins a picnic dinner and the right to spend Independence Day with the beautiful Meggie O'Day, owner of The Celebration."

The crowd of miners, shopkeepers, and gamblers murmured, then shifted as several men rushed forward to enter the race. Megan looked out over the crowd, her face reflecting some concern at the motley assortment of entrants, many of whom considered a dunk in the muddy Yukon after a winter of abstinence a sufficient bath. With an effort, she forced her "customer" smile back onto her face and waved to the assembled throng.

Alex's lips tightened. She really was playing the game for all it was worth.

The footrace was about to be run, and Alex recognized two fellow officers among the contestants. They had removed their scarlet coats and wide-brimmed hats in preparation for the competition. When they saw Alex approach, they shouted his name and motioned for him to join them. Knowing he had no choice now that he'd been seen, Alex reluctantly walked toward his comrades.

"Carson, take off your coat and get ready to run."

"I'm on duty."

"No reason we can't enjoy ourselves awhile. Come on, man, you've the fleetest feet in the force. We can't let these Yanks best us."

Alex hesitated, looking again at Megan. She had removed her hat and the sunlight reflected off her hair, causing a halo of reddish gold to hover above her head. The innocence of her expression as she smiled at the milling men below her twisted something inside his chest. She glanced over the crowd, and he saw the uncertainty of her fate in her eyes. Without pausing to question his reasons, Alex stepped forward and paid his entry fee.

His two companions laughed, pounding him on the back. Alex glanced at Megan and saw the commotion had caught her attention. She raised an eyebrow, her face reflecting amusement at his actions.

Alex turned, pulling off his jacket and hat with angry, jerking movements before taking his place at the starting line. Why he'd entered the race was a mystery to him. But since he had entered, he had every intention of winning. Then he'd tell Miss Megan-Meggie Daily-O'Day a thing or two.

The runners leapt from their waiting positions at the clang of a cow bell. Megan moved forward to lean her hands on the railing of the porch, seek-

ing a better view of the race. The course ran from
The Celebration, down Front Street, then returned
up a side street. The starting line would become
the finish line in front of the dance hall.

A thin, gangly miner who looked to be no older
than seventeen took the immediate lead. Behind
him ran a stocky-but-muscular gambler whom
Megan had seen in The Celebration on several oc-
casions. The man was obnoxious in manner and
odious in smell, and the thought of a day in his
company made her shiver. In third place she recognized Alex Carson.

Megan was impressed with the expanse of muscled chest and arms revealed through the light-
weight white shirt the lieutenant wore. Most of the
men Megan had been acquainted with were soft
and running to fat from sedentary living in saloons
and gambling halls. The obvious care Alex took
with his body created an unfamiliar stir in the pit
of her stomach.

A cheer from the crowd drew Megan's concentration back to the race. Alex moved up until he
matched step for step with the gambler. The youthful miner had increased his lead to several lengths,
while the rest of the runners fell far behind. Some
of the men dropped off to the side, walking away
from the race in favor of the cold drinks being
served from street-side vendors.

Megan craned her neck to see down the street,
and at that moment the three leaders turned the
corner and disappeared from view. She settled back
with the rest of the crowd to wait until they reap-

peared at the opposite end of Front Street. Cheers from people on the next street told of the progress of the race.

Lord, I hope that horrid gambler doesn't win, she thought. All she needed was to spend a day in the heat next to that smell. She could do without the young miner, too, for that matter. She had no desire to fend off his youthful exuberance and groping fingers. Megan looked up the street for the runners, surprised to realize she wanted to see Alex in the lead. Only as the lesser of three evils, she told herself firmly.

Three runners rounded the corner and the crowd roared. The sun shone into Megan's eyes too brightly to identify which man led the pack. The excitement of the moment caught Megan. Heat hovered and shimmered above the damp earth as the hoots, stamps, and whistles of the crowd echoed through the open air. She could smell the tension in the sweat and excitement of the multitude of observers. Everyone tilted forward, all eyes focused on the three runners pounding toward the finish line.

Megan leaned over the railing, hands gripping the wood, eyes straining to see Alex. The three men burst into the shadow of The Celebration and her heart lurched.

Alex was in second, the gambler in the lead. The miner ran fast on the heels of the Mountie. Alex's arms pumped as his powerful legs strove toward the finish line. His face was set in concentration toward the single goal of overtaking the man in the lead. Megan's hands clenched as she chanted under her breath, "Faster, faster, faster."

As if he'd heard her, Alex grimaced and shot ahead, close on the heels of the man before him; but the finish line loomed too near. He could never make it.

Megan wanted to reach out and push him forward the few inches needed to put him in the lead. In the end, Alex did not need her help. With a smile that said he had been holding back his true talent all along, Alex dove past the finish line a second before the gambler, leaving the miner to finish third.

People surged forward and she lost sight of him. Megan let out the breath she held, and a wave of dizziness rushed over her with the return of fresh air to her lungs. Someone took her arm and led her down the porch steps toward the crush surrounding Alex. The crowd parted in front of her and soon she stood in front of him, unsure of what to do.

"Your prize, Lieutenant," said the man who had rung the starting bell.

Megan's head jerked up, and her startled gaze met Alex's amused blue eyes. She opened her mouth to tell them all that she would rather dine with the devil himself than Alex Carson, but before she could utter a sound, the object of her wrath grabbed her by the shoulders and kissed her soundly on the lips.

Every word of fury she had planned to utter flew back down her throat at the touch of his mouth on hers. Alex kissed her hard and long, a kiss of victory more than passion, still the sensations reached all the way to her curling toes. If she had known a kiss could be like this, she would have tried one years ago.

But when the hoots and whistles from the crowd finally penetrated her brain, she pushed against his broad chest until he released her. "That wasn't part of the prize," she hissed at him, embarrassed at all the attention for her very first kiss.

"I don't know why not. Every winner deserves his heart's desire." Alex grinned before bowing with a flourish to the townsfolk, then retrieving his hat and coat.

Her face flamed and she put her palms to her hot cheeks. The leering smiles of the men in the crowd made her want to run and bury herself in the earth.

"If we're going to have a picnic, then let's get on with it," she grumbled as she accepted a basket of food from a shopkeeper. "I, for one, have to get back to work."

Alex leaned close to whisper in her ear. "If you put yourself up as a prize, Meggie, the least you can do is be worth the winner's effort. Shouldn't you try to look happy for me? The men might get the idea you have a cranky disposition."

Megan saw his point. After all, her entire presence at the race was intended to drum up business for the dance hall. She put on her best smile and linked her arm through Alex's.

"Now, gentlemen, if you'll excuse us, the lieutenant and I have a picnic engagement." She looked back over her shoulder and winked at the openmouthed men as she allowed Alex to lead her away.

Once they were out of earshot of the others, Alex said, "You certainly are a wonderful actress, Meggie. Did you have professional training?"

"No, but I'm learning. Give men what they want to see and hear, and they buy it every time."

He looked at her strangely. "I didn't realize you were so hard."

"Not hard, practical. Business is business no matter where you are. You just have to find the right key to open the lock of success. I think I've finally found that key with The Celebration."

As they talked, their steps took them out of town toward a small grove of pines on a hill. From their vantage point they overlooked Dawson City and the festivities. The town lay nestled between tree-covered hills, the Yukon River cutting a wide swath of blue down the center. Several makeshift sailboats dotted the water—as well as an arriving steamship. Every day more people poured into the already bursting town in search of fortune. Little did they know that all the available land had been staked for claims long ago.

With a sigh, Megan turned away from Dawson City and opened the basket, removing a red blanket that Alex quickly spread over the sun-warmed earth.

"What do you say we put aside our prejudices

of the opposite sex for this afternoon and enjoy the day?" Alex ventured.

Megan stared into his open, pleasant face for a moment before gracing him with a nod and a smile. They sat together on the blanket and companionably shared the meal.

When, a short while later, their eyes met, Megan was unable to look away from Alex's direct gaze. She had seen lust many times before in a man's eyes, but with Alex Carson the expression surprised her. She must be mistaken at what she saw in the depths of his sky-blue gaze. He was going to kiss her again; and though she hadn't expected it, she leaned forward, eager for the contact. Her eyes slid closed.

Soft, warm, feather-like, his lips moved over hers. Her chest felt as though it might burst as warm, liquid sensations pounded beneath her breast. His hand warm at the back of her neck, his fingers long and supple as they pressed her closer. The smells of summer mixed with the scent of warm male flesh, and she leaned into him with a soft moan. His tongue teased gently at the corner of her mouth, then traced a path on her slightly parted lips. Uncertain at first of what he wanted, she kept her mouth tightly closed; but as he continued to stroke her closed lips with his tongue, she sighed and her mouth opened of its own accord. She started at the first touch of his tongue on her teeth, but the sensation was so new and exciting she relaxed instantly. Tentatively, she stroked his seeking tongue with hers. She had just reached up to twine her arms around his neck and draw him closer, when her hand encountered something warm and wet and very definitely alive. With a shriek, she pulled away and jumped to her feet.

SIX

At Megan's shriek, Alex sprang to his feet, reaching for the heavy Enfield revolver each member of the mounted police carried. Without pausing to think, he grabbed Megan's arm, dragging her behind him as he turned to face the danger.

He froze at the sight of Damon, tongue lolling in a doggie grin.

"Megan." Alex endeavored to keep his voice calm. "Don't you go anywhere without your damn bodyguard?" Some of the anger he felt at being so needlessly alarmed must have seeped into his voice, because the wolf growled.

"Shut up or I *will* shoot you," Alex growled back. "Pest."

Damon cocked his head, then sat back on his haunches, panting.

"I think you're talking his language now." Megan laughed when Alex glared at her. "Don't be such a sore loser. He means well."

"Why am I always the one he exercises his good intentions upon?"

"Just lucky, I guess."

Megan placed her hand on his arm, and Alex's body hardened at the slight touch. Though he wished he could resist her allure, he covered her fingers with his own.

"We should return to the party. I *am* on duty, even though I haven't been acting like it."

Megan withdrew her hand and, returning to the blanket, packed the remains of their meal. She seemed offended, though Alex couldn't think why. A glance at the wolf showed the animal glowering again. Women and wolves, he never would understand them.

In silence they descended the hill, Damon at their heels. When they reached the outskirts of the town, the wolf trotted off in the direction of The Celebration.

"Now he leaves," Alex grumbled.

"You should be flattered." Megan's gaze followed Damon as the crowd parted to allow him a wide, clear path back to the dance hall. "I don't think he'd leave unless he thought you could protect me. It seems you've made a friend."

"A wolf for a friend. What next?"

"Why are you so irritable? Don't you feel well?" Megan turned to him, her face reflecting concern. "Maybe the heat is too much for you in that heavy coat. I think it's at least a hundred degrees today."

Could she really be so innocent that she didn't know what part of him wasn't "well" after their interrupted interlude? He found such a concept hard to believe after her cold-blooded maneuvers to make money by using her face and body. Staring down into her lovely eyes for a moment, he thought the paint she'd used to enhance her features made her look like a child playing at being a woman. Tearing his gaze from hers with difficulty, he stared down the street toward the party while he got himself under control.

To turn the conversation away from himself he said, "The heat isn't the problem, Megan. The cold will be. Just wait until you encounter a Yukon winter. You'll be begging for San Francisco before the first week is over. Maybe you should reconsider your decision to remain here."

"We're back to that again? You're becoming extremely dull."

"Well, we can't be dull with the great Meggie O'Day, can we?" Taking her arm, he pushed their way through the crowd toward the loud music at the far end of the street where a patch of flat, dry ground served as the dance floor. All of the dancers from The Celebration and the other dance halls in town danced from one man to the next. When the musicians began to play a polka, Alex pulled her into his arms and swung her into the midst of the fray before she could protest.

"Am I still dull?" he shouted over the music.

Megan faltered, and her pointed heel came down hard on his instep. Wincing, Alex continued to move in time to the music. It didn't take long for the revelation to come to him. Meggie O'Day, dance hall enchantress, could not dance a step. He fought back the urge to laugh as she attempted to shuffle her feet with the rhythm of the tune.

She tried with all her might, but after several more agonizing missteps, Alex began to count softly in her ear. "One and two and one and two and . . . That's it; keep going. One and two, and . . . We can't have the townsfolk find out that Meggie O'Day can't dance. One, and two, and . . . That would be bad for business."

When Megan didn't answer, Alex looked down only to encounter the top of her head. She continued to stare at their feet, her hand holding his in a near-painful grip. When the song ended, Megan pulled from his grasp, still avoiding his gaze.

As he looked at her bowed head, his heart did a slow roll within his chest. She tried so hard to be tough, to be Meggie, when deep down she was neither. "Thank you, Megan. You saved me a day's pay by dancing with me here rather than at The Celebration."

"I don't dance. I manage."

He had to bend close to hear the words. "Well, I thank you anyway. As I said, a dollar a dance is too rich for my pockets. How is it that a dance hall owner doesn't know how to dance?"

She glanced up at him for a moment then quickly returned her gaze to her feet as though shy. "I never had the chance for such frivolity. I've spent my life trying to keep a roof over my head and some food in my stomach, as well as my father's. Teaching his daughter to dance was never a high priority in Brian Daily's life."

The words were said without bitterness, but Alex

felt the sadness behind them nevertheless. In his quest for revenge and his hatred of her father, he had neglected to think what her life must have been like as the daughter of a wastrel.

"Where did you learn to dance?" Megan asked, breaking into his thoughts.

Alex frowned, looking out over the crowds milling through the street as he remembered. Joanna had taught him one rainy afternoon. He had been home from school in England for a rare visit, and Joanna was anxious to show off what she had learned at Grandaire's School for Young Ladies. They had spent the afternoon laughing at his clumsy attempts; but in the end he had mastered the art and earned Joanna's approval.

"My sister taught me," he murmured to Megan, still half lost in his memories. She had begun to walk back toward The Celebration and without thinking, he followed along next to her, guiding her through the thick crowd of revelers by rote.

"Where's your sister now?"

At her question, Alex straightened into a military stance. "She's dead," he said through tight lips.

"Oh," Megan's voice reflected her dismay. "I'm so sorry. Did you lose her recently?"

"Yes."

Megan hesitated. She obviously wanted to ask him more, but politeness kept her from pursuing the topic. Instead, she went on as though nothing untoward had been said. "I always wanted a sister, or even a brother. I've often wondered what it might be like to have someone else in the world you shared a bond with—parents, childhood memories. Being an only child, well, I've just been alone."

"You had your father," Alex ventured, struck by the sadness in her voice, feeling again that slow roll of his heart.

Megan smiled; but when she glanced at him, the expression did not reach her eyes. "I never really had my father for long. My mother died when I was thirteen; then I lived with an aunt for three years while my father traveled the country. Once I started traveling with him, he would stay with me only as long as it suited him; then he'd move on to his next adventure and I'd follow after selling whatever business we owned at the time."

Alex pondered how different her life had been from his with a large and loving family. He might have lost Joanna, but at least he'd had her in the first place.

Megan went on. "Sometimes I used to dream of having a family of my own, brothers and sisters to play with, to depend on if life got hard." She turned and smiled the same sad smile. "But those were only dreams. Dreams don't come true."

Alex frowned. "Of course they do. Someday you'll have a husband and children. That will be your family."

Megan shook her head. "I don't think so. That's not the life for me."

They had reached the front of the dance hall and paused at the foot of the steps. Alex turned to her, puzzled.

"Why not? All women get married."

"No," Megan said softly, "not all of them. And certainly not me."

She said the words with finality, and Alex wondered what had set her mind against the institution of marriage. He opened his mouth to ask, but at that moment someone from the crowd jostled Megan from behind and she stumbled against him. His hands came up to her shoulders to steady her, and she looked into his eyes. All other thoughts fled when he met her green gaze. His hands tightened, and he drew her closer, marveling at the softness of her skin, bared to his touch by the revealing neckline of her gown. He moved his thumbs in a light caress across her collarbone and she shuddered, then pulled away.

"I have to work tonight." Her voice was breathy, her cheeks flushed. "Thank you for the lovely day, Lieutenant."

"That's it?" he asked, unnerved at his response to her. " 'Thank you for the lovely day, Lieutenant.' Come on, Megan; when you put yourself up as a prize, a man expects more than a thank you for his money."

Her eyes narrowed at his deliberately taunting words, but she didn't answer. Instead, she skirted past him, just out of his reach, and entered The Celebration. He followed, past the surprised gazes of the bartenders in the front room, past the raised eyebrows of the dealers in the gambling room, and through the empty dance hall. When they reached the door to her rooms, she turned so suddenly

Alex stepped back. She followed and, grabbing him by the front of his coat, jerked him forward for a hard kiss, full on the mouth. Stepping away as quickly as she had advanced, Megan looked up at him defiantly. "Debt satisfied, Lieutenant."

"Not with that excuse for a kiss, Meggie." He put a sarcastic emphasis on the name she had adopted.

She grimaced at his tone. "That excuse, as you call it, will have to suffice." Before he could stop her, she slipped through the door, slamming it shut behind her.

Alex stood in the hall for several moments, rubbing his chin thoughtfully. His attraction for Megan had become a tangible ache, their day together so enjoyable he had hoped time would stand still. The memories she had shared with him of her childhood and life with Brian Daily had only served to make his feelings more tender toward her. Even her angry kiss aroused him, not to mention the embrace they'd shared on the hill. If he didn't watch himself, he might . . .

With a growl of irritation he pushed back the errant thoughts, turned, and descended the stairs to the ground floor, then burst outside into the scalding heat and sunshine of Dawson City in July.

Men were nothing but trouble. Megan knew that, always had. Just look at her father. Totally irresponsible. If it hadn't been for her looking after him, they would both have starved.

She pushed away from the door where she'd

rested her head against the cool, strong wood until Alex Carson's footsteps retreated. He had stood outside for so long, she had been afraid he was going to come in after her. Then what would she have done? She had been practicing her flirting technique each night at work and had to admit she enjoyed herself. But with Alex, the same techniques seemed foolish and out of place. The feelings bubbling to the surface within her whenever he was around confused her more than she had ever been confused in her life. Her heart pounded with anger—or was it anticipation?—at the thought of Alex kissing her the way he had on the hill earlier that day. She wrung her hands. Thoughts like that would only lead in one direction—trouble.

She had observed enough men in her life to know that women, to them, were only necessary to satisfy their own needs and wants. She had decided early on that she had room in her life for only one man, and him only because she had no choice but to honor her father. Now that he was gone— Megan swallowed back the tears that threatened to spill each time she thought of his death—she would not allow another man to use her strength to supplement his own.

As Megan went about her room getting ready for the evening's work, a tiny voice inside her head kept whispering that Alex Carson was not a weak man. He was successful in his own right. He had no need in his life for her talents in business. In fact, he was more often scornful of them than admiring. Shaking her head at the muddle her thoughts were becoming, Megan resolved to stop speculating about the handsome Mountie—at least for the coming evening. If she were lucky, the crowd for the Fourth would be so energetic, she wouldn't have time to think of anything but work.

Unfortunately, everyone seemed to have tired themselves out with the excitement from the previous night's events and the entertainment of the day. The Celebration was nearly empty, and Megan was left with far too much time to think. In the solitude of her bed the next morning, her thoughts caught up to her with a vengeance.

I should be exhausted. Instead of sleeping yesterday, I went to the festivities; then I worked all night. Why can't I sleep? She rolled over and punched her pillow with a fist. *Alex Carson, that's why. Damn him.*

He had no right to be so good-looking, and he especially had no right to kiss like the very devil. She was being unreasonable, but lack of sleep made her petulant.

Sighing with resignation, she slipped on her silk wrapper and opened the heavy curtains. Sunlight flooded the room. Since she couldn't sleep, she might as well go through her father's papers, a task she had been avoiding since she'd noticed the cluttered desk days before.

She sat in a soft leather chair in front of the heavy oak desk. The wealth of goods available in the Yukon never ceased to amaze her. If she so desired, she could go to a shop in town and buy a dress that was the height of fashion in Paris. The furniture in The Celebration, as well as in other establishments, was of the finest quality. Since Dawson City had been built on the river, any item a person desired could be obtained, eventually, by ship. With gold readily available, the merchants made the most of the opportunity by stocking every imaginable necessity and luxury.

Megan sighed as she attempted to organize the countless slips of paper haphazardly strewn across the desk. She had gone over the books almost immediately upon her arrival. Dan, the young doctor-turned-bartender whom Brian had engaged to take care of financial matters, had done a surprisingly good job. She had been astounded to learn that most of the bartenders in elegant establishments were American doctors or dentists unable to get a license to practice on British soil. Pleasantly surprised to find that her father had let someone competent handle his affairs for a change, Megan, nevertheless, had relieved Dan of his duties. She preferred to tend the finances with her own fingers. She had spent too many months in the past straightening out the tangles one of her father's associates had worked them into.

But the papers she shifted through at present were unrelated to The Celebration. She found several letters in her own handwriting, as well as letters from Brian's pals in San Francisco—men like her father, looking for an easy road to wealth. She wouldn't be surprised if several turned up in Dawson City, hoping to ride Brian's coattails to glory. She'd send them packing quick enough.

Megan's hand froze in the motion of putting

aside a paper. Drawing the document back toward her, she frowned in concentration.

What is this?

She had never seen a gold claim, nor the papers involved in registering one. But unless she missed her guess, what she held in her hand was just such a paper. She read onward in amazement. According to the paper, one Brian Daily, in partnership with Willie Shore, had registered a claim on Bonanza Creek.

Megan sat back in the chair. Papa had never mentioned a claim to her. In fact, he had made a point of mentioning that he would never work a claim but chose to make his money off those who did. And who was Willie Shore? She had never met this man or heard his name during her time in Dawson City. If her father had been in partnership with someone, wouldn't the man have contacted her? And why hadn't she heard about the claim from one of the girls or bartenders—or Queen, for that matter?

Her mind spun with the questions. More than likely, the piece of property was as worthless as most of the other get-rich-quick schemes Brian had been involved with. And this Willie Shore had probably gone back to wherever he'd come from, dead broke, as most of Brian's partners ended up.

Weariness washed over her, and she stood up. Maybe she was finally tired enough to sleep. The question of the gold claim could be resolved when her mind was clearer.

When she pulled closed the heavy draperies, the

room became shrouded in darkness once again. With a contented sigh, Megan sank down onto the massive bed and fell almost instantly asleep.

But blessed forgetfulness hovered just out of reach. Her mind haunted with images of blue eyes and auburn hair, firm lips pressed to hers and strong hands against her skin, she groaned with the pleasure. "Alex," she whispered, and the sound of her own voice tugged her toward wakefulness.

On the edge of sleep, the rustle of papers and a hint of movement nearby made Megan pull a pillow over her head. She wanted the dream back.

Suddenly the truth of what she heard penetrated and forced her toward wakefulness. Slowly, cautiously, Megan removed the pillow from her head and peered into the murky gloom. A figure stood next to the desk, quietly searching through the papers. The race of Megan's heart threatened to choke the breath from her lungs.

She couldn't just lie there and let this intruder rifle through her father's possessions. Quietly, Megan raised herself to a sitting position on the bed, eyes searching the room for a weapon. Her glance fell on the poker near the fireplace. Though the implement was several paces from her and nearer the intruder, she saw nothing else.

As she got to her feet, the bed creaked, and the dark figure whirled in her direction.

SEVEN

Megan froze, though she had to be clearly visible in the semi-darkness of the room. The intruder moved quickly; and before she could scream or run, she was shoved back onto the bed. Hands closed around her throat. She struggled, fingers clawing at the assailant, nails piercing flesh in desperation; but he was strong, and too soon black dots swam before her eyes.

As consciousness waned, Megan heard the door to her room bang open, and then the intruder fell away from her onto the floor. Air filled her lungs, welcomed though painful, and Megan's vision cleared. She heard a threatening snarl, then a startled curse from a man seconds before a heavy object hit the floor.

Staggering to her feet, Megan saw the dark figure rolling across the room as Damon attempted to gain a hold at his throat. Megan opened her mouth to scream for help but only managed a hoarse croak. She watched in horror as they rolled toward the fireplace, where the intruder grabbed the very instrument she had planned to use in saving herself. She gasped as the poker swung toward Damon and knocked the wolf to the ground, where he lay still. The assailant ran from her room, loud footsteps echoing up from the dance hall.

Megan knelt next to the fallen animal. He was only stunned, already showing signs of revival as he whimpered and raised his head to lick her hand. Petting his coarse fur, she murmured her thanks until the electric lights blared to life above her.

"Lovey, what in blazes is going on in here?"

Megan looked up to see Queen, resplendent in an orange silk wrapper, surrounded by several of the girls. Everyone turned when footsteps pounded up the stairs. The only man with a room at The Celebration, Zechariah, the bartender, rushed through the door, armed with a heavy stick. His gaze took in the dazed Damon, with Megan kneeling at his side, and he lowered his weapon.

"Right on time as usual, Zechariah," Queen drawled. "I think you girls can go back to bed now. Meggie's all right."

Amidst grumbling about lost sleep, the dancers retreated. Megan stood as Damon got to his feet, swayed a bit, then leaned against her leg.

"Miss Daily, I heard a whole lot of banging around up here, then someone ran through the hall and out the front door, right past my room. Did one of them miners try somethin' funny with you?" Zechariah peered at her closely and shook his club for emphasis. "Just tell me who and I'll take care of 'em."

"I woke up. Someone was going through my father's papers, but I couldn't see who."

"Why would anyone want Brian's papers?" Queen wrinkled her nose at the overflowing desk.

"I'm not sure, but it must have been important." Megan rubbed at the sore skin of her throat. "He tried to strangle me before Damon drove him off."

"Should I call the doctor?" Queen came farther into the room and put her heavy arm around Megan's shoulders. Damon snarled, though he still swayed as though he would fall at any moment.

"Relax, Damon." Megan reassured the animal. "I don't need a doctor, Queen. I only wish Zechariah had gotten a swipe at him."

"You'd best report this to the authorities in the mornin'," Zechariah said as he headed back to his room.

Queen stiffened then moved away. "I don't like the law, Lovey. Never have."

"Zecheriah's right. I don't want this to happen again."

"It won't. Probably just some drunk lookin' for gold. Now that he knows about Damon, he won't be back. Just make sure that beast is downstairs from now on."

"Downstairs? I think he's earned the right to sleep in my room." Megan patted the wolf's massive head before Damon trotted over to flop onto the carpet, closing his eyes with a peaceful sigh.

When she looked up, Queen had disappeared. *That's odd,* Megan thought. *And I wanted to ask her about the gold claim, too. There's always tomorrow.*

She climbed into bed and, despite the upsetting events of the night, fell immediately into a deep sleep.

Alex grimaced when he drew duty in the office for the next week. He really couldn't complain, since he hadn't worked there since his arrival in Dawson City. But he had always hated office work, and he detested the task even more since he had other places to be and people to question in regard to Joanna's death.

The morning dragged as the heat mounted, and the air inside the small office building matched the temperature outside degree for degree. Alex tugged on the collar of his uniform and sighed. This was going to be a long week.

The door swung open and Alex glanced up, then came to his feet in a rush at the sight of Megan and Damon. The scent of just-cut lemons permeated the heavy air, and Alex breathed deeply of the cooling fragrance. Today she wore a frock the color of summer sunlight. The shade flattered her, though Alex had no liking for the seductive style she had adopted with her transformation.

"Were you looking for me?" he asked, annoying himself with the hopeful lilt to his voice.

Megan seemed uncomfortable at finding him in the offices of the mounted police. She wrung her hands, glancing at the door with longing before swallowing and meeting his eyes with a challenging glare. "Not you in particular. I'd like to report an assault."

Alex clenched his teeth. Some drunken sot of a miner had tried to get fresh with one of the girls, no doubt. Motioning for Megan to take a chair, Alex did the same as he picked up a pen. "The woman who was assaulted should be here, not you, Megan. Which one of the girls is it?"

"Not one of the girls. Someone attacked *me* in my room last night."

"You!" He jumped to his feet, hands clenched. Now that he looked more closely, what he'd thought were shadows from the room were actually light bruises about her neck. Who had dared to touch her?

"I'm all right." She smoothed the fur on the wolf's head. "Thanks to Damon."

"Who was it?"

"If I knew the answer to that question, I wouldn't be here. I was sleeping; and when I awoke, I saw someone rifling through my father's papers. When I tried to stop him, he attacked me."

Alex's eyebrows drew together in confusion. "I would think a thief would look for gold, not personal papers."

"I had the same thought. But if not gold, then maybe this." She withdrew a paper from her sleeve and handed it to him.

As he took the missive from her outstretched hand, he noticed the length and fragility of her fingers. Images of those soft hands on his face, neck, chest shot through his mind.

"Lieutenant?"

Megan's questioning voice brought him back to

reality, and he opened the paper with a snap. He had never had a problem keeping his mind on his work before Megan Daily entered his life.

The document was the title to a gold claim in the names of Willie Shore and Brian Daily. He looked up at Megan. "What's this?"

"That's the only item of value I found when I went through my father's papers again this morning. Do you think that's what the intruder was looking for?"

Alex rubbed his chin thoughtfully. "Perhaps. Though the claim belongs to whomever it's registered to, or their heir in this case, not who's in possession of this paper." He glanced at the document again and frowned. "Who's Willie Shore?"

"I was hoping you might know. I asked Queen, and she had no idea my father even had a gold claim, let alone a partner." Megan smiled fondly. "She was mighty put out that he'd kept something from her, too."

"I can imagine." Alex returned her smile as he handed the paper back to her.

"Is there any way to find out more about this Willie Shore and the claim?"

"I'll ask around; but if Queen doesn't know him, I can't say that I'll have much better luck. As for the claim, the directions are right here on this document. You can go take a look at the land for yourself if you'd like."

"I suppose I'll have to. Will you take me?"

Alex started at her question. He had convinced himself in the early hours of the morning that fur-

ther contact between himself and Megan Daily
should be kept at a minimum. He was attracted to
her far too much for his own peace of mind. But
he found himself wavering at the beseeching look
in Megan's clear green gaze.

"I suppose I could take you there on Sunday. I
should really check this claim myself, as it's related
to your assault." Alex prided himself on the businesslike tone of his voice. Too bad his heart was
hammering in a very unbusinesslike rhythm.

"Sunday would be perfect. Thank you."

Megan stood and snapped her fingers to
Damon. Alex admired the sway of her hips through
the thin fabric of her dress as she walked toward
the door. When she turned, he hurriedly shifted
his gaze to her face.

"What did you do with the dog?"

"Dog?" Alex wondered if he had missed part of
the conversation while he was admiring her nether
regions. He cleared his throat and coughed to
cover his embarrassment.

"The puppy we rescued the other night. I forgot
to ask about him on the Fourth." She looked up
at Alex from beneath her lashes. "The day was a
bit hectic."

Alex recalled their interrupted kiss on the hill.
Studying her closely, he saw evidence of a blush
upon her cheeks. If he didn't know better, he'd
think Megan Daily had never been kissed before.

"Ah, yes, the pup." He faltered, forgetting for a
moment what he'd done with the animal. "I gave
him to a friend. Don't worry, he's in good hands."

"What friend? I'd like to see him sometime."

"Ah, I gave him to a miner—a miner who left for his claim yesterday. He might be back here in a few months. I'll let you know." He hoped his hastily constructed tale would convince her to let the subject drop.

Megan stared at him for a moment longer, then smiled. "Yes, let me know. About the pup and about Sunday."

She exited the office, leaving a hint of lemon fragrance in her wake, and Alex released the breath he had been holding as he fell back into his chair and grimaced. Women, wolves, and pups were nothing but trouble.

The following Sunday, Megan was dressed and waiting on the porch of The Celebration before any of the girls were awake. She hadn't seen Alex since that morning in the office, but he had sent a note telling her to be ready at noon, dressed for riding and minus her wolf, who would spook the horses.

Megan smoothed the material of her black riding habit with its split skirt, then adjusted the brim of her matching flat-topped hat. She thanked her lucky stars she had learned to sit a horse as a child and continued to ride whenever possible. The terrain around Dawson City was rough, and she would need all her skill to reach her father's claim.

The sound of hoofbeats neared, making her squint into the noonday sun. Alex Carson approached on horseback, leading another horse behind. As always, he wore the uniform of the mounted police. She wondered, momentarily, what he would look like in anything else.

Alex drew his horse to a stop in front of the dance hall. Jumping to the ground, he stood at the foot of the stairs and tipped his black hat. "Your mount awaits, my lady."

"Thank you, kind sir." Megan accepted his help getting onto the mare, ignoring the tingle at her waist when his hands touched her. She smiled at him from her perch in the saddle. "How long will it take us to reach the claim?"

"A few hours. Are you up to this?"

"Certainly, Lieutenant. I'm as ready as I'll ever be."

She watched him remount, admiring the flex of his muscular legs and the obvious strength in his large hands. She guided her horse into step beside his as they left town.

"It's hard to believe the temperature will start to drop by the end of this month," Alex remarked. "There's been snow as early as August in these parts."

"I'll have to enjoy the sunshine while I can."

"We all do in the Yukon. The sun will disappear in mid-November and you won't feel its warmth again until late January."

Despite the warmth of the day, Megan shivered. The thought of everpresent darkness for months on end was daunting.

"Ready to head for sunny California, Megan?" Alex taunted.

In response, she straightened her spine and lifted her chin. "Not on your life, Lieutenant. With things starting to go my way in Dawson City, I can handle darkness, cold, and anything else this country hands out."

"I thought you'd say that. Did you inherit your grit from your mother's side of the family?"

Megan stiffened again, sensing the veiled slight to her father. "No. My mother was a quiet woman of poor health. Father was the adventurer. He taught me everything I know."

"Let's hope not," Alex muttered.

"What is it with you and my father?" The volume of her voice startled a bird from a nearby tree. She watched it fly into the expanse of blue then returned her attention to Alex, lowering her voice and reining in her temper. "You've made several comments about him; I get the feeling you knew my father and didn't like him. Am I right?"

"No, I never met Brian Daily, but I've heard many things."

Megan frowned. "I don't understand."

"Did Brian come to Dawson City alone?"

Confused at the change in subject, Megan hesitated before answering. "Of course. He left me in California with our restaurant."

"He didn't bring along a friend, a lady friend?"

"No. He's never had any lady friends that I know of. I think losing my mother broke his heart." Alex snorted and Megan's anger rose again. "Are you ever going to tell me why you detest him so?"

"People aren't always as they seem." Alex stared off into the distance. "Especially those we love. We see them the way we want them to be, not the way they truly are."

The sadness in his voice caused memories of Megan's life with Brian to surface, and without thinking, she shared them with Alex. "I suppose you're right in some ways. My father left me with my aunt after my mother died. When he came back and took me on the road with him, I hoped it was because he'd been lonely without me. He did love me, but he took me along because he'd seen I was capable beyond my years. He would leave me behind, in charge of whatever business he'd begun, then move on to the next town, sending for me once the new business was established but in need of a solid hand in management."

"Sounds like you were a business asset, not a daughter."

His putting into words what had always remained hidden in her heart, caused Megan to hesitate for a moment before blurting out the truth. "Sometimes I felt just like that. I would wake up one morning; there'd be a note, and he'd be gone. I used to cry for days after he left, until I realized that crying wouldn't bring him back. The only thing that would make my father love me was being a better manager than he could ever hire."

She shook off her melancholy. Why was she telling Alex these things? He already had a poor opinion of her father; she didn't need to add to that impression.

Megan forced a smile and a laugh. "But my life was never dull. I'm a strong, capable woman because of him, and that's a rarity in this day and age."

"It's a shame you spent your girlhood at work. You should have been having fun, going to parties, not playing at spinsterhood."

"I'm good at my job. I don't miss having those things in my life. I'm happy."

"Are you?" Alex continued to stare at her. "I wonder."

"Well, don't." Megan's smile faded. She didn't need his curiosity, or his pity. "If you want to wonder about something, wonder who this Willie Shore is. Do your job."

"I know my job." He looked away. "I find it odd that no one knows anything about Willie. If he's a miner, or was one, he should have been seen in town at one time or another."

That bothered her, too. It was as though the man had never existed. But he must have, since his signature was boldly written on the registration to the gold claim.

Alex crested the hill ahead of her and stopped his horse. Megan pulled hers up next to him. Below lay Bonanza Creek, birthplace of the Klondike gold rush. She could see several rough dwellings along the river, most merely rough shelters against the wind. She had heard that most of the creek was mined out already and many of the claims abandoned. The eerie silence up and down the river gave credence to that rumor.

Alex broke into her thoughts. "If we ride upstream a bit, we'll find your claim."

Megan nodded and followed him as his horse picked its way down the rock-strewn hill. A few moments later they stopped and Megan surveyed her unknown legacy.

There wasn't much to see, though her father's claim looked better than most. A rough wooden cottage stood at the bottom of a hill several hundred yards from the creek. A lean-to had been added to the rear of the building, firewood stacked next to it.

"I'll take a look inside." Alex dismounted. "Why don't you look around out here."

Megan nodded and got down from the horse as Alex walked away. She watched him until he disappeared into the building, then meandered to the creek's edge.

Sunlight shot sparks off the surface of the water, and she bent to dip her hand into the flow. The cold shot from her fingers to her wrist in a painful jolt. Glancing around, she spotted a shiny object several feet away on the bank of the creek and she hurried to pick it up.

Megan turned the rough metal pie plate over in her hands as she examined it. She had seen enough in Dawson City to know a mining pan when she found one. The miners used them to sift through the sand at the bottom of the creek. The gold would settle and the finer sands would wash out with the water.

She continued to stare at the pan for a moment

as the realization came to her. Someone had been mining this claim. Since her father was dead, that someone must be the mysterious Willie Shore. If not him, then a thief was about.

Without warning, her arms were grabbed from behind and yanked behind her body. Her cry for Alex was silenced when a gag tortured her mouth, and the sunlight became darkness as a heavy burlap sack descended over her head.

EIGHT

The cabin was cool, dry, amazingly well kept—
and empty. If Alex had to make a guess, he would
say someone had been here in the past week.

A faint, muffled cry from outside caught Alex's
attention and he went to the door to see if Megan
had found something. His glance swept the riverbank and surrounding area.

"Where has she gotten to now?" He walked
around the cabin in search of her. A movement at
the edge of his vision made him glance toward a
small band of pines several yards away. Alex narrowed his gaze and caught again the slight rustle
of branches. He hurried in the direction of the
trees. "Megan?"

His answer was the whistle of a bullet over his
head.

"What the hell?" Alex ducked behind the near-
est tree and drew his weapon.

He peered around the tree trunk; and when
nothing happened, he crouched low, running to a
tree farther into the grove. When no more shots
were fired, he continued the process. Ahead, he

heard the unmistakable sound of rustling boughs
and retreating footsteps. Whoever had shot at him
was on the run.

Praying Megan was somewhere safe, Alex continued his pursuit. Soon he caught a glimpse of two
figures ahead, one pulling the other along and
knew his prayers had been in vain. Megan was not
safe; she was kidnapped.

He sighted his pistol above their heads and
pulled the trigger. At the sharp retort, Megan stumbled, then fell to her knees. Her kidnapper hesitated, then ran, leaving Megan sprawled on the
ground.

Alex raced to her side and ripped the sack from
her head. Her green eyes filled with fear until she
recognized him. "Stay here; I'm going after him."
She nodded and Alex left her untying the gag se-
cured around her head.

He hadn't run far when another shot forced him
to take cover. Ahead he could see the end of the
trees and two horses waiting beyond. But every
time he attempted to leave his secure location, a
bullet made him return to hiding.

When Alex heard the snort of a horse he ran,
pausing before he left the cover of trees. Just crest-
ing the hill, a large, cloaked figure sat astride a
horse, leading another horse behind. Open ground
lay over the hill, and he had no chance to catch
a mounted man. By the time he returned for his
own horse, the kidnapper would be far and away.
With a sigh, Alex holstered his pistol and returned
to Megan.

He found her leaning against a tree, rubbing her mouth thoughtfully. "Are you hurt?"

"Just a sore mouth and a skinned knee. What happened?"

"He had two horses waiting on the far side of these trees. I'm fast but no match for a horse."

"Did you see who it was?"

"No. What about you?"

She shook her head. "I found a mining pan near the creek and was looking at it when I was grabbed from behind. I didn't see anything until you pulled the sack from my head."

Alex stared in the direction of the hill over which the kidnapper had disappeared. "Something very strange is going on here, Megan. First you're assaulted in your own room, now this. I don't like it."

"Couldn't it be coincidence?" Megan's voice and her face were full of hope.

Alex stopped and looked down into her eyes. "I hardly think so. Nothing happened until you discovered Brian had a gold claim. This place is the key to the man in your room and the kidnapping attempt today. The same person is probably behind both incidents."

Unable to stop himself, Alex ran a finger down Megan's dirt-smudged cheek. She looked so vulnerable and frightened, the urge to protect her returned.

He didn't realize he'd moved closer until her breath whispered past his cheek. "What should we do?"

He ignored the question and kissed her instead. She stiffened with a gasp of surprise. Using both hands to cup her face, he deepened the kiss, and the gasp turned into a sigh. Megan's hands linked around his neck and her body swayed toward his.

Alex forgot where they were, who they were, what had just happened in the pleasure of their kiss. He outlined her mouth with his tongue, and when Megan's lips parted he delved inside to taste and stroke. His hands left her face to slide down her arms, then span her waist. How could she be so soft, yet so firm?

His lips trailed slowly from her mouth, across the fine line of her jaw to her ear. When she threw back her head with a moan, Alex feasted on the delicate flesh of her throat. Her hands clenched on his upper arms, showing she felt the same inner fire as he.

"Maybe we should go back to the cabin," he murmured near her ear.

At his words she stilled then pulled back, pushing at his chest, and he cursed the gentlemanly instinct that had kept him from tumbling her there on the ground.

"Whom do you think you're dealing with, Lieutenant?" she hissed. "I am not some tart to be had for the taking, be it on the ground or in a cabin. You'll have to search elsewhere for such diversion."

Alex fought to get his breathing under control. Her hand shook where it rested at the top button of her riding habit, and her eyes looked impossibly huge and dark in her pale, dirt-smudged face. Her lips, red and swollen from his kisses, trembled. She was either a very good actress, or a scared young woman after her second passionate embrace. Alex found the latter hard to believe when he remembered who she was and what her life had been like before he'd met her.

Straightening to his full height, he bowed, then walked stiffly back to their mounts. She followed, sharply refusing his offer of help.

They returned to town in silence. But the incidents of that day, as well as of the previous week, had raised new questions in Alex's mind and he resolved to find the answers upon his return to Dawson City.

After Alex had escorted her back to The Celebration, Megan accorded him a cool thank-you for his help, then left him standing in the street. In the quiet of her room, she paced, angry at herself for allowing her emotions to override the reason they had gone to the claim in the first place. She had been so upset over the kidnapping and the shared embrace among the trees she had neglected to ask if he had found anything inside the cabin.

An image of Alex kissing her, his hands on her body, and her response flashed through her mind, and she stopped her aimless pacing to stare into space. How dare he! What was it about the man that could so infuriate her one minute and excite her the next? If the meaning of his words had not penetrated her mind, she would have gone with him to the cabin without argument. There he would have proved her the type of woman she insisted she was not. Then where would she be?

Megan fell onto her bed and stared at the ceiling. She'd be his mistress, that's what. She'd seen what happened then. The woman ended up mistress to a string of men, each one exceedingly worse as the woman's health and beauty waned, until she was forced to earn her living as a prostitute or take her own life in escape.

The door to her room opened and Megan leapt to her feet.

"Relax, Lovey, it's only me." Queen sashayed into the room, lowering her bulk into a chair.

"Queen, do you think you might knock before you come in next time?"

"Whatever for? You'd just tell me to come in. I'm saving time, that's all."

Megan rolled her eyes. She'd learned quickly that there was no arguing with Queen. The woman would have her own way regardless of what anyone said.

"Did you want something in particular, or did you just miss me?" Megan asked.

"Did you have fun with that handsome Mountie?"

"I wasn't supposed to have fun. We went to look at Papa's claim."

Queen sat up straight at the mention of the gold claim. "Did you find anything interesting?"

"A mining pan near the water and fresh wood stacked near the cabin. We didn't get a chance to look around much more since someone thought it would be a good day to kidnap me."

"Kidnap you? What for?"

"I don't know. But Lieutenant Carson feels that today's incident and the one the other night must be related. I suppose he's right."

Queen looked at her closely. "Is somethin' else botherin' you?"

"Like what?"

"I just wonder if that Mountie is too much for a young thing like you to handle."

"I can handle him."

"Hmm. Anything you want to ask me about? Maybe how things are between a man and a woman?"

Megan turned away, blushing. "I don't think so, Queen."

"Well, I was just wonderin'. What with your ma dyin' young like that and Brian bein' the way he was, I don't figure anyone explained things to you."

"I know what's supposed to happen, Queen."

"I'm not talkin' about what goes where, Lovey; I'm talkin' about the art of makin' love. The way you're actin', I think that young man's got you scared to death."

Megan remained turned away from her friend. She had no desire to share such personal feelings and fears with anyone. Besides, after the way she had rejected Alex at the claim, she doubted there would be any more incidents between them that she didn't know how to handle.

"I'll be fine." Megan walked to her father's desk and hunted through the scattered papers.

"What're you searchin' for?"

"The claim paper. I thought maybe I overlooked something when I read it." She began to shift the mess more frantically as she realized the paper was not on the desk where she'd left it. "I put it right on top; I know I did."

Megan ran quickly to her night table, pulled open the drawer, and looked inside. Then she got down onto her knees and peered under the bed and around the floor. When she bumped into a pair of violet slippers, she looked up to see Queen standing over her, hands perched on ample hips.

"What are you doin' down there?"

Megan sat dejectedly on the floor. "Someone's taken the deed." She spread her hands in a gesture of helplessness. "Why? The paper is of no value."

"Your guess is as good as mine. If the deed's not important, then don't worry about it." Queen shrugged and prepared to leave.

"It's not the paper I care about but the fact that someone's been in my room again. I thought Damon would discourage any visitors."

"The wolf comes and goes as he pleases. You can't expect the animal to stay inside day and night. It's not natural."

Megan sighed. "I suppose not. But the thought of someone touching my things, stealing from me . . . I won't stand for it, Queen."

Queen, on her way out the door, paused and

looked back. "You don't need to get your dander up with me. I'm on your side."

Megan smiled at the woman she had come to think of as a friend. "I know, and I appreciate your help. If it weren't for you, I'd be out on the street by now."

"I doubt if the situation was that desperate. Someone would have helped you if I hadn't. See you later." With a flick of her brightly painted nails, Queen disappeared from view.

"You have more faith in human nature than I, my friend," Megan murmured.

She spent the next half hour scouring the room for the claim paper. Then she spent another hour asking the dancers and bartenders if anyone had been near her room. When both approaches yielded no clue, she sighed and went in search of Alex. Despite her desire to avoid him, she knew she must report the theft and further invasion of her privacy.

After rousing Damon from his nap on her bed, Megan slipped out the front door and made her way toward the headquarters of the Mounties, the black wolf trotting at her side. Since it was the Sabbath, all businesses were closed until 2:00 A.M. Monday by decree of the mounted police. The streets were nearly deserted. She remembered how the claim had seemed deserted, yet someone had been stalking her. Looking down at Damon, she felt safer for his presence and loyalty.

Suddenly the wolf stopped, head cocked to the side, and a thread of fear ran through Megan's chest. She strained her ears but heard only the usual sounds of a Sunday in Dawson City. The nape of her neck tingled and Megan whirled around.

No one was there.

Glancing at Damon, she saw his attention focused down an alleyway to their right. The narrow avenue led to the next street—Paradise Alley. As though scenting a rabbit, the wolf put his nose to the ground and ran down the alley.

"Damon, where do you think you're going?"

In answer, he stopped and looked over his shoulder, tongue lolling from his mouth, as if to say, "Come on, this will be fun;" then he continued on his way.

With a cautious glance up and down the street, Megan followed her wolf into the shadows.

Somewhere along the way, Alex had lost his perspective. Sea-green eyes, silky red hair, and luscious peach lips were no excuse for forgetting his duty to family.

Immediately upon returning from the trip to Megan's claim, Alex went to Paradise Alley and questioned again the prostitutes working there. Unfortunately, the women living now in the broken-down shacks had not yet arrived in Dawson City when Joanna had died. His sister had the dubious distinction of being one of the first prostitutes in the Yukon.

After hours of questions with no answers, Alex wearily knocked at another shack. But this time, instead of with wary curiosity, he was greeted with genuine pleasure by a petite, dark-haired woman. Her face, once beautiful, was now lined with strain and ill health. Her dress was frayed, and many launderings had faded the color beyond recognition.

"Baby boy, come on in here and visit. Get down, Brainless." The woman attempted to control the yellow puppy as it tried to climb Alex's leg.

"I see you've found a name for my gift. I hope he's not too much trouble, Geraldine." Alex made himself at home in a chair and glanced around the one-room building. He tried not to flinch at the knowledge that Joanna had spent her last days in such squalor. He had met Geraldine the first day he had come looking for his sister.

"The pup's no trouble," Geraldine said, "though he eats like a horse. I enjoy the company. What brings you here so soon after your last visit?"

"Discouragement. I've been up and down Paradise Alley again, and no one knows anything about Joanna or Brian Daily. Someone, somewhere, must have seen them together. Or if not him, then another man. I can't understand how I keep coming up with nothing, no matter how many people I question." Alex dropped his head into his hands, and Brainless promptly slobbered all over his face.

Geraldine knelt and pulled the pup into her lap, then she sat on the floor in front of Alex. "I'm sorry as can be about Joanna, but don't you think it's time you admitted she's gone? You can't change that fact. Get on with your life."

"You know I won't rest until I find out why she

left home and how she could have committed suicide."

"I can't tell you any more than I already have. I moved into this place a week after she was buried. She kept to herself and did her job from what I heard. Hell, no one found her until one of her customers got curious and walked in. She could have been swinging for a day or more."

Alex winced at Geraldine's words, and she put her hand out to gently touch his knee. "Sorry, baby, my mouth gets away from me sometimes. Forgive?"

Alex sighed and covered her hand with his own. "Of course. You've been the best kind of friend, Geraldine. I'll never be able to repay you for all your help."

She shrugged her thin shoulders and smiled. "Forget it. Having you visit and talk to me like a human being keeps me from going crazy."

"I've told you before, I'll give you the money to leave here."

Geraldine withdrew her hand from his and stood. "No, I am what I am. Can't change a tiger's stripes, and you can't change me no matter how hard you try."

Alex stared at her for a long moment, then got to his feet. "I'll come back when I can."

"You're always welcome. Just don't bring me any more pets, you hear?"

"I won't. I found myself saddled with that one despite my better judgment."

"I heard how you saved the pup—and Meggie

O'Day, too." Geraldine's searching gaze swept his face.

"What, exactly, did you hear?"

"The girls tell me you're been keeping company with her. I'm not surprised. She's the belle of the ball, as they say."

"Well, you can tell the girls I'm not keeping company with anyone. Our encounters are strictly business."

The memory of Megan's soft, enticing curves pressed to his body flashed through his mind, but he pushed the traitorous thought away and refused to entertain any others.

"Strictly business, huh? I'd heard she wasn't in that kind of business. Look but don't touch, she says, and that wolf makes sure the men toe the line."

"That's right, and I can toe that line as well as anyone." Alex pulled open the door and stepped into the evening sun.

"Don't get your back up. I was just curious."

Geraldine sounded hurt, and Alex turned back, putting his hands on her shoulders and leaning down to kiss her quickly on the mouth. "I know and I'm sorry. I don't want to talk about Meggie O'Day right now." He patted the pup where it slept in her arms. "I'll have our cook send over some scraps for Brainless."

"Thanks. Don't be a stranger, hear?"

Alex waved and nodded, touching her gently upon the arm before turning in the direction of his barracks.

* * *

Megan watched in disbelief as Alex Carson emerged from a hovel on Paradise Alley. When Damon would have run forward to greet his new friend, she hissed for the wolf to stay and be silent. Ignoring the animal's reproachful look, she peeked from the alley at the scene in front of her.

A woman emerged from the house. Alex seemed to be angry at first, then Megan's mouth fell open when he leaned over and kissed her. He patted the golden puppy in her arms, and Megan's lips tightened when she recognized the dog they'd rescued on the night of the fireworks. He said he'd given the animal to a friend. Megan wasn't so naive that she didn't know what kind of friend he was talking about now. Before he walked away, Alex touched the woman tenderly on the arm.

"Lying, hypocritical, bast—" Megan muttered through her teeth. "And he has the nerve to preach to me."

Spinning on her heel, she snapped her fingers to Damon and marched back to The Celebration, reciting what she would say to Lieutenant Alex Carson the next time he showed his face at her door.

NINE

Three o'clock on a Saturday morning and the patrons of The Celebration were in full swing, making merry before the enforced day of rest. Over the past weeks, the dancers had come to accept Megan—if not as one of them, then as someone to be trusted to keep their best interests at heart.

She sat at a table in the dance hall and watched the show. Several young miners hovered around her in hopes she would consent to dance with one of them that evening. She never did. Megan knew that part of her allure lay in the fact that she wasn't like the other girls. She didn't dance—no matter what they said, no matter what they offered. And she knew that even if a young, handsome face with the gold to back up his lies tempted Meggie, Megan Daily couldn't dance a step to save her soul.

In the middle of an animated conversation with the miner to her right, she felt the crowd stir. As she turned her head slowly toward the door, her eyes met Alex's, and he smiled as though he were genuinely glad to see her. *And he calls me an actor,* she thought before turning her attention back to the man beside her.

Alex strode up to her table and within minutes dispersed the circle of admirers with a few well-aimed scowls.

"That's better," he said, as he took the seat closest to hers.

"For whom?" she asked coldly. "I was having a pleasant conversation until you showed up."

"With that group of infants? I never thought you had the makings of a governess, Megan." Alex smiled and took her hand. "I wanted to apologize for the way I acted the last time we were together. I'm sorry I didn't come to tell you sooner. Can we pretend that never happened?"

For a moment Megan thought he'd seen her spying on him outside the hovel on Paradise Alley and her shoulders tensed. Then she realized he meant the kiss at the claim. She hadn't thought of the incident in two weeks. Well, maybe only once or twice.

"Certainly, Lieutenant. I can easily pretend it never happened since I've already forgotten the incident."

She must have put just the right amount of nonchalance into her voice because he removed his hand from hers. The loss of his warmth saddened her for a moment, until the image of him kissing that woman came to mind. Gritting her teeth against her damned attraction to Alex Carson, Megan resolved to give him a piece of her mind.

"I came looking for you that Sunday," she began.

"You did?"

"Yes, I had something important to tell you."

"Did you come to the office?"

"I was on my way, but an interesting sight sidetracked me."

"What?"

"You—and a friend."

Immediately his eyes became cold, his face distant. "Oh? I don't have many friends here."

"I distinctly remember your telling me you gave the puppy to a friend. I saw you with a woman, and she had the puppy. Interesting coincidence, don't you think?"

He didn't answer but stared at the dancers on stage as they finished their last show of the evening.

"Lieutenant, I'd love to know why you're so against a woman earning her living as a—" She paused and put a finger to her temple as though searching for the appropriate word. "—a soiled dove, shall we say? Then I see you kissing a bird of the same feather on the street in broad daylight."

"It's always daylight here at this time of year," he grumbled, still staring at the stage.

She waved her hand in the air. "Oh, so you couldn't help but kiss her in daylight then. You, sir, are a hypocrite."

Alex didn't answer and Megan felt a twinge of unease. She had been hoping to goad him into telling her the truth, certain he had an excellent explanation for his whereabouts and actions of the afternoon in question. But his continued silence and cold demeanor made her wonder if she had pushed him too far over something that was truly none of her business.

After several more moments of silence he turned and grabbed her hand in a tight clasp. Megan stifled a cry of pain, her gaze riveted on the anger mixed with anguish in his blue eyes.

"I think it's time you learned some truths about your father, Megan."

"I know all I need to know. He's dead, Lieutenant; why do you hate him so?"

"He may be dead, but his passing was much too painless to suit me." Alex pulled her hand so she had no choice but to lean toward him. His next words were but a whisper, yet she heard them very clearly. "Brian Daily murdered my sister."

Megan wrenched her fingers from his and stood, knocking the chair over in her haste. "You must be mistaken."

"You're perfectly welcome to prove me wrong." Alex smiled without humor, leaning back in his chair to look at her.

Megan drew in a deep breath and glanced around the room. Several of the young miners had seen their heated exchange and frowned at Alex. Not wanting trouble or an audience, she forced a smile and resumed her seat.

At his puzzled glance she whispered, "You'd do

well to keep up appearances while we discuss this or *we* might have a brawl on *your* hands."

His eyes swept the room, taking in the angry looks from the throng. His gaze returned to her face and he nodded his understanding.

"Now," she said, "start explaining."

"My sister Joanna ran away from home two years ago. I wasn't there at the time." Pain haunted his eyes before he took a deep breath and continued. "My parents said she had a misplaced notion of becoming a singer. I tracked her to San Francisco, where she had sung in a saloon." Alex yanked at the collar of his uniform with his free hand. "By the time I got there, she was gone. The owner of the saloon said she met a man, and when he went off to the Yukon, she disappeared along with him. One of the bartenders told me the man's name— Brian Daily."

"And what did Brian Daily look like?"

"Tall, thin, scholarly. With red hair and a blonde mustache. Always wore a pencil behind his ear, mumbled a lot, and scribbled in a notebook."

Megan's heart thudded in time with every word he uttered. Alex described her father exactly as she remembered him—always full of ideas and always afraid he'd forget the best one if he didn't write it down immediately.

She shook her head against the memories. "Just because my father was seen with your sister doesn't mean he murdered her. Did anyone see them leave San Francisco together?"

"No. But they were on the same steamer to Seattle and arrived in Dawson City the same month."

Megan made an impatient sound deep in her throat. "So what, Carson? That's nothing."

"I'm not through yet. Once she got to Dawson City, Joanna continued to sing." He paused and looked directly into Megan's eyes. "At The Celebration."

"And then?"

"Then things get complicated. No one seems to remember when or why she left here, but she turned up next as a prostitute on Paradise Alley." He gazed at a place above and to the left of Megan's shoulder. "She hanged herself two weeks before I arrived."

Megan swallowed and reached for his hand. "How awful for you. I'm sorry." She was silent for a moment, thinking of how horrible he must have felt, arriving too late but so very close to saving her. "But if she killed herself, my father couldn't have murdered her."

"From what I can piece together after talking with some of the women on Paradise Alley, she had just found out she was expecting a child. When she told the father of the child, he immediately took her to that hovel and disappeared."

"Then look for the father."

"The only man she was ever seen with was Brian Daily. He disappeared the day after she showed up in Paradise Alley, and then he was reported dead in the avalanche shortly after. Joanna killed herself the day after word of the avalanche reached Dawson City."

They sat in silence, thinking about his words. Finally, Megan spoke. "I think you're allowing your grief and your anger to guide you, rather than the facts. I know my father. He wouldn't hurt anyone. If he were involved with Joanna, I'm sure he planned to return and take care of her."

"Then why did he take her to that—" Alex grimaced with disgust. "—that place? Why did she kill herself? Why did she leave a note saying life wasn't worth living without the father of her child?" He put his head into his hands and muttered, "Why, why, why?"

Something tightened in Megan's chest as she witnessed his pain. She smoothed the auburn hair falling over his forehead, letting the strands play through her fingers, relishing the softness as she fought the urge to pull his face to hers and . . .

His head came up and he stared into her eyes. The blue of a tropical ocean had become a river in winter and she withdrew her hand from his hair.

"I'll find out if Brian was the one; and if he was, I'll make sure The Celebration is dismantled board by board."

Staring into his eyes, she knew he meant to carry out his threat. But she also knew her father, knew he wasn't capable of the kind of deception this man accused him of. Now all she had to do was prove it.

Pretending to ignore his threat, Megan asked calmly, "Doesn't Queen know anything about this?

She seems to know everything about everyone else."

"Queen isn't talking, at least not to me and not about Joanna."

Megan frowned. "She has to know something. She's worked here since the place opened. She must have known Joanna."

"She knew her. But according to Queen, Joanna kept to herself and talked to no one except Brian."

"I'll talk to her. Maybe she'll tell me something."

Alex looked doubtful. "Why would she?"

"I don't know, but I don't plan to let you condemn my father and take away my place without a fight. Whether you like it or not, Lieutenant, you've just acquired a partner."

July gave way to August and the air turned frigid. Megan had a seamstress make up several dresses in heavier fabrics, although still in the same revealing styles. She compensated for this by ordering heavy shawls as well.

The Celebration was busier than ever with the miners trying to get in as much fun as they could before ice and snow bound them to their cabins for weeks or months on end. Megan rarely found time to pursue her questions regarding her father, Joanna Carson, and the claim on Bonanza Creek. She saw little of Alex, who was also kept busy with the increased traffic in town.

In her free time, Zechariah taught Megan to play poker. She found she had a natural aptitude and spent a good portion of her evenings dealing in the gambling room. Her presence there increased their take on the tables, and she found the nights passed more quickly with something to occupy her hands and mind.

On a cold, damp night in late August, Megan dealt the last hand of her turn at the tables. So intent was she on the game that she failed to notice the man behind her until he slapped her on the back and roared in her ear.

"Little girl, you look mighty fine. Who dressed you up for the party?"

Megan jumped at the stinging slap and the volume of Big Ian McMurphy's voice. She had hoped that with the obvious improvement in business at The Celebration, he wouldn't bother to darken her dance hall again. But her luck in that regard had run out. Glancing quickly at her cards, she threw them onto the table.

"Gentleman, I fold. It's been a pleasure."

When she stood, all the men around the table jumped to their feet. Smiling, she collected her winnings and handed them over the bar to Zechariah. Only then did she face Ian.

"To what do I owe the pleasure of your company, Mr. McMurphy?"

Ian guffawed and slapped his knee. "The pleasure of my company. Ain't that rich?"

The gambling hall had gone quiet as each man strained to hear what was being said while pretending to continue his game. She stared at Ian without smiling. After a moment he stopped laughing and cleared his throat.

"Well, I've decided this place doesn't suit me after all. I plan to take over Jerry's Place down the street real soon. Givin' you some competition, little girl."

Megan hid her wince at the mention of competition, though she knew her dance hall could hold its own with the likes of Ian McMurphy. Keeping her face blank and her voice light, she answered, "The Celebration doesn't suit you? Or maybe it's just too rich for your blood now that I've made the place a success?"

"I have to admit business has picked up real fine since the last time I came by. You look a mite different, too. If I'd've known you looked so womanly under those drab fixin's, I would've grabbed you for myself." Ian frowned. "Heard that Mountie's been sniffin' around your skirts."

Megan opened her mouth to refute his crude statement, then thought better of it. If the rumor that she was seeing Alex Carson kept Ian away from her, all the better.

Megan sighed. "Why are you here, McMurphy?"

Ian's gaze had wandered past her and focused on the dance hall. He seemed not to have heard her and Megan called his name, none too softly.

The big man's attention returned to her momentarily. "Just thought I'd be neighborly." He straightened his shirt and swept the coarse, black hair from his eyes. "Um—aah—might you know where Queen is?"

So, that's the way of it, Megan thought, suppressing a smile. She marveled every night over Queen's undeniable allure to the opposite sex.

"She's in back. You're welcome to pay your dollar like the rest of them, Ian."

Without further comment, Ian McMurphy strode from the room into the fading strains of a violin's song. After a moment's thought, Megan followed him. As she'd expected, Queen was surrounded by men requesting her first dance. For such a large woman she was surprisingly agile, and her personality drew men like flies to melted sugar.

At Ian's approach, the crowd of admirers parted. When he waved a fistful of dollars in their faces, the men retreated. Megan had to smile when she saw Queen's chagrin. Nevertheless, she snatched Ian's money, placing it carefully in her bodice before he swept her onto the dance floor.

They were deep in conversation, and Queen looked fit to be tied. Her mouth opened and closed quickly with her tirade, but Ian merely smiled at her fondly. He was obviously besotted with the dancer. If Megan didn't miss her guess, The Celebration would be short its most profitable employee within the year. Despite her distaste for McMurphy, she hoped Queen would find happiness.

For the past month Alex Carson's life had been a mesh of days without sleep, meals on the run, and constant duty. But tonight, things had gone quiet and he was going to The Celebration to see Megan.

Stepping from the brisk August air into the subdued warmth of the building, he saw her immediately. She wore one of her "Meggie gowns," as he thought of them, her hair loose and curling, held back from her face with a purple ribbon. His fingers itched to yank the bit of fabric from her redgold tresses and taste her mouth until the torment in his body ceased.

She looked up and saw him then, and for a moment the look on her face said she felt the same as he. Then the mask she wore with all the customers slid into place, and she came forward with a practiced smile. "Lieutenant, what brings you here? I thought you were patrolling another portion of Dawson City this month?"

"I'm not on duty."

The fresh lemon fragrance surrounding her caused the usual response in him. Silently he cursed his treacherous body and strove to keep his thoughts from showing on his face. Taking Megan's arm, he led her to an empty table at the back of the saloon. The customers and her employees watched, but he ignored them all.

"We need to talk," he said.

"Certainly." She moved closer. "Have you found out anything more?"

When she leaned over, her low-cut dress presented him with a view of her breasts he hadn't previously been privy to. He stared, then stuttered, his mind a blank. "M-more about what?"

Megan noticed where his eyes were focused and sat up abruptly, frowning. "About my father, your sister, the claim—anything at all?"

Alex cleared his throat and glanced around the room. Several pairs of curious eyes shifted their focus upon encountering his gaze. Returning his attention to Megan, he said, "I haven't had much time to question anyone. How about you?"

"Nothing new here, either. Queen insists she knows nothing, as do the other girls. I talked with Zechariah, but last year is a blur to him."

Alex sighed in frustration. "I have one more person I need to question, but that may be a problem."

"Why?"

"Because this person and I don't care much for one another, to put it mildly."

Alex's attention was caught by a flurry of movement in the doorway. Big Ian McMurphy ducked and entered the front bar.

"Speak of the devil," he murmured.

Megan followed his gaze. "Ian? You think he might know something?"

"I intend to find out." Alex stood and placed himself directly in Ian's path.

Ian walked with his head down, mumbling angrily to himself. "Damn, blasted, woman. What the hell I see in her, I'll never know."

"McMurphy."

The big man's shaggy head came up and he scowled at Alex. "Not now." He attempted to push past.

"Now. I have a few questions and you've been avoiding me."

Ian continued to scowl, but Alex stood his ground and pointed to a nearby table. With a growl, McMurphy threw himself into a chair. "Make it quick."

Alex glanced at Megan, who hovered about, and jerked his head for her to retreat. She did, though with obvious reluctance. He didn't want Ian to think anyone was listening to their conversation. People talked more freely if they thought their words were confidential, and Alex needed all the help he could get with this man.

"You came to Dawson City around the same time as Brian Daily."

"So?" Ian's voice was belligerent.

"Did Daily arrive with a woman?"

"I wasn't here when he arrived. Didn't meet him till he opened this place a few weeks later. Why?"

Alex ignored the question and posed another of his own. "Did you ever meet Joanna Carson?"

"Who? Never heard of her."

"She was a singer here. Called herself Sweet Josie."

"Oh, her. Killed herself, didn't she?"

Alex was immediately alert. Very few people in Dawson City paid attention to the lives and deaths of the women on Paradise Alley. Ian seemed to know more than most. Covering his excitement, he answered, "Yes. Did you know her?"

"Not personally, if you know what I mean." Ian raised his eyebrows suggestively.

Alex fought the urge to lunge across the table and choke the man. "I was told you came in here quite a bit when the place first opened. That you and Brian played a lot of poker."

"So, what's the crime in that? Brian was good company."

"Did he ever mention being involved with Joanna?"

"Josie?" Ian's brow creased with the effort of thought. "Now that you mention it, he was kind of partial to her. Bought her little presents all the time and talked sweet, ya know?"

Alex was silent for a moment, strangely sad at the further confirmation of his belief. He had found himself hoping recently that Brian Daily was not involved in Joanna's death.

"Anything else, Carson?" McMurphy stood.

"Not at the moment But I'll want to talk to you again."

"If you can corner me." Ian left the dance hall laughing.

Megan took the vacated seat. "What did he say?" Hope brightened her eyes.

The hope did him in. She truly loved her father; and though Alex thought Brian Daily the worst type of scoundrel, he didn't have the heart to hurt Megan with what he'd learned.

"The trail is cold. I can't do anything more." He rose, planning to make his exit before Megan saw through his lie.

Before he moved a foot, she took his arm and

spun him around angrily. "What did he say?" she
hissed.

"He didn't know her, Megan."

"You're lying. He said my father was involved
with your sister, didn't he? You still think he abandoned her and the baby." She shook his arm, fin-
gernails digging into his flesh. "Believe what you
wish. If you can't prove he left her, I'll prove he
didn't."

She exited the room in a flurry of velvet, petticoats rustling with indignation. Alex had no doubt
she would try to prove him wrong. He hoped, for
both their sakes, she could.

TEN

The following day, the streets of Dawson City were lined with people. An early snowfall had arrived several days before, dusting the ground with just enough of the white powder to make a sled dog race possible. The crowd's mood was festive as they waited for the dog team race of the year to begin.

Ian McMurphy and Jerry Stone each owned a prize team of sled dogs. Since a single dog cost as much as three-hundred-and-fifty dollars, a year's wages for a man in the states, it was a measure of the two men's wealth that each owned an entire troupe. For months, each had boasted that his team was the fastest and strongest. The time had come to find out. The race was set for a Sunday so all the sporting folk could watch and gamble on their day off.

The Northwest Mounted Police were not amused. They had threatened to arrest those involved if any such race occurred on the Lord's day. Ian and Jerry were willing to take that chance. Jerry had bet his dance hall while Ian was throwing his largest saloon into the pot.

Megan fastened a cloak around her shoulders, took one last look in her mirror, then shrugged. She spent at least an hour on her appearance each day before leaving her room. For a woman who had never done more than twist her hair into a bun and wash her face, such frivolity had fast become onerous. But she had learned that appearance was more than half the game, and she played the game well, though the longing for a simpler time, a simpler self, never left her.

Earlier that morning, Queen had relayed a message from Ian requesting that Megan drop the handkerchief to start the race. Knowing her visibility in front of crowds was good for business, Megan agreed, though she regretted the loss of a day without petticoats, pins, and prying eyes. At the rate life was passing by, she would be an old woman before she had a moment to herself.

A cheer from the crowd outside told her the dog teams were taking their positions. She hurried from the room and through the echoing dance hall, high heels clicking across the wood floors.

Her dancers and bartenders had taken up residence on the porch while waiting for the race to begin. Final bets were placed and the odds favored Ian's dogs.

Megan declined a chair along with a chance to throw her money away on one of the teams and hurried to the opposite end of Front Street, where Ian awaited her.

"Been waitin' on ya, little girl," Ian said impatiently.

"I'm here. Let's get this over with."

Craning her neck to see past Ian's massive form, she viewed several Mounties standing at attention. Her gaze settled on Alex Carson, but he continued to stare ahead, giving no indication he was aware of her regard.

"Been told they'll arrest everyone involved for gamblin' on a Sunday," Ian said. "But the race has to take place before they can do it." He rubbed his hands together. "By then I'll be the owner of a dance hall."

"Do you really think they'll arrest *everyone?*" Megan didn't want to find herself in jail within the hour.

"Nah, they're just bluffin', tryin' to prove who's in charge." Ian escorted her to the starting line. "Let's get to it, Meggie."

Pulling a white handkerchief from her pocket, Megan held the cloth aloft for a long moment, then released it. A cheer went up from the crowd as the lead dogs lunged forward in response to the whips cracking above their heads.

Megan's attention was diverted from the race as the line of Mounties moved forward. She backed into the crowd quickly, planning to return to The Celebration before the group could arrest her or anyone else. If she put Damon on guard outside her door, maybe they would leave her alone.

A hand shot through the crush of people and grabbed her arm, jerking her backward. Turning around quickly, she slammed into a red-clad chest with such force the breath flew from her lungs.

"If you have to break the law," Alex drawled, "the least you could do is be less conspicuous about it."

Pushing futilely against the hard expanse of him, Megan said, "I didn't think the Mounties would be so concerned over a little fun. Are you really going to arrest everyone?"

Alex looked down at her and smiled. He rubbed his thumb over her ice-cold cheek and the contact warmed her to her toes.

"Not everyone. That is if I can get you back to your place before anyone sees us."

Megan's eyes widened. "You'd do that for me?" He didn't answer, just pulled her along down a narrow side street. "Won't someone notice I'm not in jail? I was a bit on display back there."

"I'm betting the jail will overflow with prisoners, so no one will notice. If they do, they won't care. Inspector Starnes plans to put all the men to work chopping wood on the Mountie woodpile anyway. They'd just let you go with a tongue-lashing."

With the townspeople's attention on the race and the Mounties' attention on the townspeople, Megan and Alex reached The Celebration without being stopped.

"Do me a favor and stay inside, out of trouble, for the rest of the day. Do you think you can manage that?"

"Certainly." Alex started to turn away, but

Megan put a hand on his arm. "Thank you for helping me. You didn't have to."

He covered her fingers with his own. "Yes, I did."

Megan searched his eyes, but shouts from outside drew Alex's attention and he looked away before she could interpret what she saw in his gaze.

"I have to go. But I'll come back tonight and we'll talk."

"I'll be waiting."

Alex gave a short nod and left. Megan shut her door, moving across the room to the window and pushing aside the heavy curtain to look down at the street. Seconds later Alex appeared below, striding purposefully toward the commotion without looking back.

Megan turned her head, pushing her cheek up against the glass window in an effort to get a better view of the crowd. The dogs still raced down the center of the street while the mounted police arrested anyone they could grab from the sidelines. Those not being accosted by an officer escaped hurriedly down the side streets and alleys. From Megan's vantage point they looked like nothing more than ants scurrying for the cover of their anthill. She chuckled at the thought, then realized she would have been one of those ants if not for Alex Carson.

What would he expect from her by way of thanks?

The race was over, but the excitement had only begun. Alex spent the rest of the day dragging people to the mounted police offices where they could be sentenced to their term on the woodpile. He thought the entire exercise a waste of time, but he was trained to follow orders. His conscience twinged on occasion at the thought of how he'd disobeyed orders by helping Megan escape. Such an action was totally out of character for him.

Late in the day, angry words from the office drew Alex's attention. Recognizing the voice of Ian McMurphy, he hurried inside.

"I'm gonna shoot every one of them animals. Ran like a herd of pregnant moose. Did ya see 'em?"

Several of the Mounties nodded, obviously having heard this tirade already.

"So, you lost your saloon, McMurphy? I'd say that's justice, wouldn't you?"

The big man swung around like an angry bear awakened from a winter sleep. "If you meddlin' Mounties would mind your own business, life would be a lot simpler in Dawson."

"Maybe so, but we're here to stay." Alex smiled with satisfaction. "How long will we be enjoying your talents on the woodpile, Ian?"

A growl of rage shook the room; and before he could react, Alex lay on his back with Big Ian straddling his waist. "You're more trouble than that scrawny sister of yours ever was, Carson."

A large, meaty fist barreled toward his face, and Alex raised both his elbows to ram them sharply into Ian's chest. The man fell backward, enabling Alex to roll to his feet. He waved the approaching

Mounties away. He would handle this fight on his own. As Ian tried to climb to his feet, Alex brought his clenched hands down onto the back of Ian's neck. The big man collapsed like a house of cards and lay on the cold floor in a stupor.

"Lock him up." He motioned to two new recruits and they dragged McMurphy away. Only when he'd caught his breath did Ian's taunt about Joanna register in his brain.

Glancing at the door through which Ian McMurphy had disappeared, Alex cursed. He would have to wait several hours before he could question his adversary again.

Megan spent the rest of the day and evening in her room, lounging in her bath, taking a nap, reading a book while she scratched Damon's ears. But no matter what she did, images of Alex Carson pushed aside all other thoughts. When would he return—after the show or maybe closer to morning and the end of his shift?

The Celebration would reopen at two A.M. so Megan crossed to a shoulder-high Oriental screen in the corner of the room and slid behind it to dress. After Queen had burst in on her for the sixth time when she wore nothing but her unmentionables, Megan had attempted to purchase a lock for her door. In a town where everything was available for a price, locks were sold out. As a compromise, she'd purchased the screen and ordered the lock.

Untying her ivory velvet robe and throwing it

over the screen, Megan bent to pull on her stockings. When a knock sounded on the door, she called "come in," wondering why Queen had suddenly acquired manners now that Megan dressed behind the screen. Finishing with the stockings, Megan ran her fingers through her hair, then tossed the heavy mass back as she straightened.

"Queen, can you help me into this dress?"

"I'd rather help you out of it."

Megan let out a startled squeak at the sound of Alex Carson's voice. Damon growled once at the sound, but subsided when he saw who had entered.

"Traitor," Megan grumbled at the wolf. She looked at Alex. "What are you doing here?"

"I told you I'd be back later." He moved closer and Megan crouched lower behind the screen.

"I'm in my . . . aah . . ." Megan floundered for a way to say "underclothes" without mentioning the word. Finally she gave up. "Move back."

"I thought you needed help."

"Not from you. Why are you in my room anyway?"

"Did you or did you not tell me to come in when I knocked?"

"Not you. Queen."

Alex looked around the room. "She's not here."

Megan ignored his obvious amusement at her predicament and said bluntly, "Leave. I'll be downstairs as soon as I'm dressed."

"I like the view in here much better." He eyed her bare shoulders and unbound hair with appreciation.

She let out a small, strangled sound. "This is ridiculous. Get out or I'll have Damon make you go."

Alex cast a glance at the wolf, now sleeping peacefully on her bed with his nose tucked under his tail. A soft snore hovered in the air.

"I don't think he's up to it today." Alex crossed the remaining distance to the screen.

Megan let out a squeak, grabbed her dress, and held the garment in front of her in an attempt to cover her nearly unclothed form.

"Get out!"

Alex knocked aside the flimsy screen and pulled Megan close. "You owe me a kiss, Megan. And I've been thinking about little else since the last time I held you in my arms."

She struggled; but as his head dipped toward hers, she realized she had only succeeded in dropping her dress to the floor. Her movements ceased when their lips met, and further thoughts fled.

Alex had kissed her before, but never like this. His tongue thrust into her mouth, and he crushed her semi-clothed form to his chest. The buttons on his uniform bit into her flesh through the thin material covering her skin, but the magic he worked with his mouth and roving hands made the minute pain recede.

Her hands moved from Alex's chest to his neck, drawing him nearer as her tongue warred with his. She felt his fingertips skim her ribs and move upward to cup her breasts through the material of her undergarments. She moaned as he rubbed his palms over the already hardened buds of her nipples. Then his hands moved down quickly to cup her buttocks and pull her to him. Her thighs cradled his arousal and, despite the fear these new sensations aroused in her, she pushed closer still.

Alex tore his mouth from hers, bending and lifting her into his arms. Her head fell against his shoulder as she fought to catch her breath. Beneath her ear, the hammering of his heart attested to Alex's passion.

"Sorry to interrupt, Lovey," Queen drawled from the door.

Alex dropped her feet to the floor and they turned to see Queen grinning at them.

"Dammit, Queen, can't you knock?" Alex growled.

"No." Queen and Megan spoke the single word simultaneously, one amused, the other angry.

"What do you want?" Alex asked as Megan dove for the robe lying atop the collapsed screen. She jerked the sleeves over her exposed arms and tied the sash as tightly as she could.

"There's a woman downstairs asking for you, Lieutenant. Says her name is Geraldine." Queen wrinkled her nose. "Looks like one of them from over on the Alley."

Megan turned away. How could she have forgotten about the woman Alex had kissed? He had never answered her questions about that day.

"Tell her to wait, Queen; I'll be right down." Alex's voice broke into Megan's thoughts.

She heard the door close behind Queen but

didn't turn around, continuing to stare at the wall. Alex came up behind her, placing his hands lightly onto her shoulders.

"Who is she?" Megan asked softly.

"A friend. I've told you that before."

"And what do you tell her about me, Alex? Am I your friend, too? How many friends like us do you have in Dawson City?"

Alex turned her to face him, his fingers tightening on her shoulders. "That's uncalled for, Megan. What's between us and what's between Geraldine and me are two very different things."

"Are they really?" Megan frowned at a sudden thought. "What exactly is between us, Alex?"

He made an impatient sound and swung away from her. "I can't discuss this with you now. If Geraldine came here looking for me, it must be important. I'll come back once I've found out what she wants."

Megan continued to stare at him, trying to decide if he told the truth. Alex departed without another word or glance, and she was left feeling she didn't know him at all.

But that wasn't the thought frightening her so deeply. After the way she had reacted to his kisses, his touch, she knew herself even less.

ELEVEN

Geraldine stood just inside the front door of the saloon, looking as though she would bolt back to Paradise Alley at any second. Alex took her arm to lead her outside.

"I'm sorry I had to come here, baby boy. I know you aren't supposed to be seen with me, but I heard something today I thought you should know."

"Don't worry about me," Alex soothed as they walked down the street arm in arm. "What did you hear?"

"One of the girls came by. She remembers meeting your sister once before she died."

Alex frowned. "I thought all the girls here now came after Joanna died."

"Well, mostly they did. But this one was here for maybe a week. She'd been told not to tell you anything."

"By whom?"

"Now I can't tell you that. Can't tell you who the girl is either. She'd scared to death as it is. But she felt bad lying to you and she knew we were friends, so she came to me."

Alex sighed in exasperation. He'd had a feeling something was being hidden from him when he was asking questions. "What did she say?"

"She said your sister had a friend named Willie Shore. Not a customer, mind you. Just a friend. No one ever saw the guy, but Joanna talked about him a lot. Right fond of him she was."

"Willie Shore," Alex muttered. "Great." He should be happy to find another link between Brian Daily and his sister. Instead, his heart sank.

"Do you know him?" Geraldine asked.

"I've heard of him."

Her face brightened. "Then maybe this will help."

"Maybe. The only problem is a lot of people talk about Willie, but no one seems to have seen him. He's been quite busy for a man who never showed his face in town."

They reached Geraldine's shack and she turned to face him. "I'm sure you'll find what you're looking for. I just hope you don't get in trouble with the Mounties or Meggie O'Day because I came to find you."

He looked at her sharply. "Megan has nothing to say about it. As for the Mounties, they may not approve of us consorting—" He made a face at the word. "—with the women here, but we're friends and I choose my own friends without the benefit of anyone's opinion. I appreciate your bringing me the information."

"Any time." Geraldine opened her door and immediately a flash of yellow fur bounded through to run headlong into Alex's boots. Brainless landed in a tangle of feet, legs, and ears on the ground, and Alex couldn't help but laugh.

"I wonder sometimes if he has bad eyes," Geraldine remarked as she gathered the pup to her ample chest. "He runs into walls and chairs all day long."

"I can take him somewhere else if he's too much trouble."

"Not on your life. We understand each other, Brainless and me."

Alex left Geraldine cuddling the dog and made his way back to his barracks. He spent the rest of the night trying to figure out the connection between Willie, Brian, and Joanna and wondering what course of action he should follow next.

Megan paced the room in her tightly laced dress, not even bothering to change after working all night. She was too angry to sleep.

How dare he kiss her that way, make her feel things that were so wonderful and new, then walk out with another woman—and just the type of woman he berated her for being?

She paused and bent to yank off her high-heeled shoes. With a flick of her wrist she sent them sailing across the room to hit with a satisfying thump against the wall. Damon jumped up from the bed to growl menacingly at the shoes.

"Oh, shut up," she snapped, sinking to the floor in a pool of satin. Seconds later, a cold wet nose pushed against her ear. She patted the massive head. "I'm sorry, boy. It's not you I'm mad at. Go back to sleep. One of us should get some rest."

Megan went to the window and gazed out at another bright, warm day. The perfect kind of weather to be outside. If she couldn't sleep, maybe a visit to her father's claim was in order. And she didn't need any *Mountie* to take her.

Shortly thereafter, dressed in her riding habit, Megan instructed Damon to remain in her room. Though she would have liked to bring him along, he would spook her horse. She went downstairs to pack a lunch for her trip. When memories of her previous visit to the claim surfaced, she slipped a long, wicked-looking knife into the picnic basket.

She reached a nearby stable and rented a horse for the day. Within a few hours she would be at her father's claim. If Alex Carson could no longer be bothered with her or her questions, she would just have to take care of them herself.

The day was spectacular, the warm breeze and deep-blue sky a startling contrast to the snow-covered ground. The last time she had made the trip, wildflowers had bloomed against the shimmer of the day's heat.

Two hours later, Megan crested a hill. The cabin lay below, seemingly deserted. Remembering just how wrong she had been the last time she'd thought that, Megan approached with caution. After circling the area on the horse, she dismounted and walked toward the cabin. Stepping inside, she saw that the dwelling was as empty as she'd hoped.

Megan put her picnic basket on the table, then

drifted around the room looking for something, anything, that might tell her if her father had lived here or who his mysterious partner might be. But if Brian Daily had once been in the small cabin, he had left nothing of himself for his daughter to discover. The place was as impersonal as a hotel room.

A flash of white on gray caught her eye, and she turned toward the fireplace. Crossing the room, she bent for a closer look. A charred piece of paper lay amidst the ashes and Megan frowned, wondering how Alex could have missed what looked to be a letter, or if someone had been in the cabin since her last visit.

The light inside was not conducive to reading, so she stepped outdoors and squinted at the nearly illegible scrawl on what was left of the letter.

Bria she read between the burned edges. *Meet you at the base of Chilkoot Pa*

The rest of the letter had been burned away, but the scrawled signature bore an unmistakable resemblance to the name *Willie.*

Megan frowned. Her father had died on the way to the base of Chilkoot Pass. Though no one could have predicted an avalanche would occur while he was descending, the letter gave her an odd chill. She'd just about had it with the mysterious Willie, too. When she found the man, she'd shake him until she had the answers she craved.

A shadow passed over the sun and an icy wind rustled the paper in her hands. Megan glanced up to see black clouds dancing across the sky, rumbling in the direction of Bonanza Creek. The wind whipped the tops of the trees surrounding the cabin until they slashed against each other with a hissing tune. Her horse whinnied and pranced with unease, tossing his head against the tether as he snorted at the coming storm.

As the first flakes of snow whistled past her cheek, Megan sighed. She would not make it back to Dawson City that night.

"Where is she?"

Queen raised her eyebrows, then lifted a huge—and surprisingly shapely—leg from a huge bathtub, pointing her toes toward the ceiling. Water dripped from her heel.

"Who might that be, Lieutenant?"

"You know damn well, who. Megan. She's not in her room and no one's seen her all day."

"You think I know where she is? She's my boss, not the other way around."

Alex stifled the urge to shake the information out of Queen. Such a tactic would involve pulling her from the water, and that was a sight he wasn't ready to see.

"Just tell me where she is and I'll get out of your way."

"Who said I wanted you out of my way? It'll do wonders for my reputation to have it known Lieutenant 'Ice-in-his-Veins' Carson busted in here while I was in the tub. The longer you're here, the better for me."

Alex swore and slammed out of the room, the

echo of Queen's laughter following him down the stairs.

He had awoken that morning with the realization he hadn't returned to talk with Megan as he'd promised. He could only imagine what she'd thought after he'd left with Geraldine and never come back.

He had stopped by the jail on the way to The Celebration and been greeted with the news that Ian McMurphy had spent his hours chopping on the pile and been set free. When he went to Ian's place it was to be told the big man had left town for an indeterminate amount of time. The news did little to improve his mood.

Now Megan had disappeared. His initial fury was fast being replaced by unease. The only thing keeping him from calling in the rest of the force in the Yukon was the fact that Damon rested comfortably on Megan's bed. He knew no one could have taken her from her room by force with the wolf on guard. So, wherever she had gone, she had gone there on her own. But what had happened once she left The Celebration was anyone's guess.

"Lieutenant?"

Alex's head came up sharply at the sound of his name. Zechariah, Megan's aging bartender, beckoned with a gnarled finger.

"Be you looking for Meggie?"

"Have you seen her?"

"Not since this mornin'. She tripped out of here early with a picnic basket on her arm. I figured she had a date, so I didn't say nothin'. But since

I figured she had a date with you, and you're here . . ." He shrugged. "Didn't want to get you riled up, Lieutenant."

"Which way did she go?"

Zechariah went to the door and jerked his thumb toward a large barn in the distance. "To the stables. Thought you two might be meetin' in the hills, if you know what I mean." He winked. "Anyway, she rode out toward Bonanza Creek."

Alex sighed as his gaze took in the rapidly darkening sky. He could only hope she'd made it to the cabin safely. Still, he'd have to go after her. With a freak snowstorm, there was no telling how long she could be trapped in the cabin, if she had been lucky enough to make it there at all.

"Get the kitchen to pack as much food as a horse can carry, as well as blankets, bandages, and brandy. I'll be back as soon as I get my horse."

"Do you think Meggie's okay, Lieutenant?" Zechariah's lined face creased even more with worry.

"That's what I mean to find out."

The whinny of a horse woke Megan from a sound sleep. She blinked, uncertain where she was for a moment, but a second whinny had her sitting upright at the table where she'd dozed off. Her heart pounded as her fingers searched out the knife she carried in her skirt. Who was outside?

A thump in the lean-to was followed by the low-voiced tones of a man. Megan's fingers clenched the knife, panic lodged deep in her chest. When the door swung inward, she jumped to her feet and moved behind the cookstove. Unfortunately, her hiding place obscured her view of the door.

She waited for a glimpse of the intruder. Seconds later, a cloaked figure came into view. Megan slipped around the stove, knife at the ready as she crept forward. She was almost close enough to place the knife at his throat and demand an accounting for his presence in her cabin, had even raised her hand to do just that, when the figure whirled, grabbed her wrist, and twisted. Her cry of pain mingled with the clatter of the knife hitting the floor.

"Is that any way to greet your savior, Megan?" Alex Carson asked, jerking her against him.

The breath left her body as he pressed her to the hard, muscled length of him. She felt the cold dampness of the snow on his clothes reaching toward her skin through the cloth of her riding habit.

"What are you doing here?" she gasped.

"I came to get you, though it looks like we'll be stuck here now."

Megan's gaze flicked to the open door. Snow fell in a constant stream onto drifts the height of a horse. Closing her eyes for a moment, she sighed. Now she was truly in trouble—snowbound with the only man who had ever made her feel like a woman. The thought brought her eyes open with a snap, and she realized Alex still held her against him. She pushed away and after a moment's hesitation he allowed her to go.

"How did you find me?" she asked as she moved back to the relative safety of the fireplace.

"Zechariah saw you go to the stables and you told the owner where you were going. If you meant for this to be a secret, you went about it all wrong."

Her earlier fear swelled within her. "You think anyone followed me?"

"Not in this storm. I barely got here."

"How did you?"

A bit of snow melted and ran down his cheek. He gave it an impatient swipe. "Finding stranded citizens is my job, ma'am."

"I'm not stranded."

"Yes," He shrugged free of his wet cloak and spread it over a chair near the fire. "You are."

When he turned back to her, Megan's breath caught in her throat. She had often wondered what he would look like without the uniform of the mounted police. Now she knew—and she was in even deeper trouble than she had imagined. His blue flannel shirt covered him adequately enough, except for the V of flesh revealed through the three buttons unfastened at the top. There Megan could see smooth, bronzed skin covered with a light dusting of auburn hair. The flannel was worn and soft looking and stretched tightly across the expanse of his chest and arms. His denim pants were also worn, just enough to mold around his strong thighs and buttocks.

Megan's gaze jerked up to his, and she found

he watched her with a small smile and raised brows. "Seen enough?"

Megan's face flushed with embarrassment and she ducked her head. What had gotten in to her? She was staring at Alex Carson the same way the men at The Celebration stared at her. She hated those stares, though she tolerated them for business reasons. Yet here she was looking at Alex as if she wanted to tear off those clothes and see what lay hidden beneath. She stifled a groan at the unruly direction of her thoughts.

"I'm going to bring in the supplies."

Alex's voice from the door brought Megan's head up from her mortified contemplation of her toes. He smiled at her and she nodded. There was nothing she would have liked better than to be left alone. If only for a few minutes.

By the time Alex returned with his saddlebags, Megan's cheeks had returned to their normal shade and temperature and she had talked herself out of her sudden and unnerving attraction to denim and flannel.

"What did you bring?" she asked, pleased with the coolness of her voice.

Alex glanced at her strangely, but the amused smile she thought she saw lurking on his lips disappeared at her glare. He cleared his throat and coughed. "Food, medical supplies, and blankets. We're set for the long haul."

"Trust a Mountie to be prepared."

"*Preparation* is my middle name. Can I interest

you in dinner? I worked up quite an appetite trudging through that snow."

"I'm interested in dinner, but only if you can cook. I never graduated beyond ordering in a restaurant."

Alex looked nonplussed for a minute at the idea of a woman who didn't know how to cook, but he shrugged and began to rifle through his saddlebags.

"I've become pretty adept at moose stew since I was assigned to Dawson City." He moved to the stove and glanced back over his shoulder. "Sound all right?"

"Anything's fine."

Her stomach rumbled in agreement, reminding her she hadn't eaten since the night before. Megan settled back on the fur and watched as Alex prepared their meal with his back to her. He definitely knew his way around a stove, and she couldn't complain about the view either.

Alex threw unknown items into a stew pot. "Why did you come up here when a storm was brewing?"

Megan quickly shifted her gaze to the fire before he caught her staring at him again. What was wrong with her? "I . . . ah . . . there wasn't any sign of a storm when I left."

"This time of year a storm can come up at any time. You should never travel away from town alone, Megan. It isn't safe."

Alex stirred the contents of the pot, clapped a lid on top, and left the stew to simmer before joining her on the rug. His knee brushed hers as he settled on the floor, and Megan shivered from the contact, instinctively inching away.

"I know that now." She stared at the fire, anything to keep from looking into those blue eyes. "I just wanted to get away."

"From me? From what I make you feel?"

Her breath struck in her throat as she continued to stare at the fire so desperately her eyes stung, then watered. The snow hitting the door seemed loud in the too-silent room, and a crack from the roaring fire made her jump and gasp. When his finger touched her chin, gently turning her face to him, she met his eyes and slowly nodded.

"I won't hurt you," he murmured, right before his lips touched hers.

His kiss was just as she remembered it, yet so much more. She didn't understand how he could be gentle and ruthless at the same time. Tentatively he stroked her lips with his tongue; and when she opened her mouth, he boldly dipped inside. With a moan, she let her hands roam up his arms, following the path her eyes had traced when he entered the cabin.

Alex pulled the pins from her hair, and it cascaded around them as he lay her back onto the fur, bracing himself on his forearms above her as he continued to assault her mouth with his.

He was wrong, she thought. He could hurt her—hurt her unbearably if she let him get too close. She knew better than to allow a man to capture her heart. She had seen the effect a so-called "love affair" had on a woman. If love were involved, then why did everyone always end up so unhappy in the end?

Megan listened to the voice of reason whispering in her head; but when his lips and his hands touched her, she found herself powerless to resist. *Just a little longer,* she pleaded with her conscience. *Allow me just a little more of this bliss, and then I'll end it forever.*

His lips left hers and traveled across her cheek; then he nuzzled at her ear. His hands moved over her shoulders, kneading and smoothing the tense muscles. The warmth of the fire combined with the heat building inside her to make a near unbearable inferno. He unbuttoned the shirtwaist of her riding habit, and the air upon her heated skin felt heavenly. When his lips followed the path of his fingers, she arched to greet them.

"I know you want me as much as I want you," he said against the tender, untouched skin at the edge of her corset. "Let me make love to you, Megan."

Megan froze at the word *love.* It was as though the warning her mind had whispered to her seconds earlier had come alive. Alex wanted to make love to her, but she knew what he felt, what they felt, had nothing to do with love. She might be naive as to what actually occurred, physically, between men and women, but she knew about the ruined lives lust left in its wake.

She stiffened within his embrace and he lifted his head to look into her eyes. "What's wrong?"

"I—I—can't."

He frowned into her face for several moments, then disentangled himself from her. The loss of his warmth and touch was a physical pain. He stared at the bare skin revealed by her unbuttoned bodice, and she sat up quickly, refastening her clothes with trembling fingers.

"You *won't* is what you mean." Alex sighed. "I don't understand you, Megan. I want you and you want me. What could be more natural than that?"

Megan paused and glanced over her shoulder at him. He now sat with his back to her, staring into the flames, his head bent in such a way that he reminded her of a confused child. He was right. Whenever he touched her or kissed her, she could hardly remain standing from the riot of sensations he aroused in her. Did she want to remain ignorant all her life of what lay between a man and a woman? Up until she'd met Alex Carson, most men had repelled her. She might never have another chance to be with a man she was physically attracted to.

Megan turned and reached out a tentative hand toward Alex's broad back.

"After all," he muttered, as if to himself, "it's not as though you're a complete innocent."

Megan's fingers froze, inches from his shoulder. Then, slowly, achingly, she withdrew her hand and turned away.

TWELVE

Overcome with a need for fresh air, Megan left Alex staring into the fire and went to the back door. When she opened it, a blast of cold air and snow slapped her in the face and several inches of snow fell onto her stocking feet. She squinted against the whiteness and, finding no sanctuary in the storm, she slammed the door shut.

She ignored Alex and dragged a chair nearer the stove, her mind swirling with the implications of his muttered words. After all the time they'd spent together, after all the times she'd told him that she wasn't a whore, he still believed the worst of her. In the face of his prejudice, the truth of her innocence was almost laughable. She had spent so many years fending off unwelcome advances as her heart hardened against all men but her father, that she had stopped believing in love and forever after and made herself self-sufficient. Then she'd discovered one man who made her burn with a need for the things she'd scorned, only to find that he was no different from the rest.

A footfall alerted Megan to Alex's approach. She

stiffened but did not turn around. He paused behind her chair.

"I've made you angry again." He put his hand on her shoulder.

Megan turned around, shrugging his hand from her body. "Don't."

Alex raised his hands in a gesture of surrender. "All right. Hands off. But could you do me a favor and keep the same rules for longer than a day? Ten minutes ago you wanted nothing more than my hands all over you; now I can't touch. Megan, you're making me insane."

She stood and faced him. "Fine. You want rules. I'll give them to you. No more kissing. No more touching. No more talking to me about anything but business for as long as we're here. I can't throw you out in the storm, as much as I'd like to, but I don't have to be insulted in my own cabin."

"Insulted? Since when are you insulted by a man being attracted to you? You have hundreds fawning over you every night at The Celebration and you thrive on it. Why am I different?"

Megan bit the inside of her lip to keep from screaming at him to get out of her sight. He had just confirmed her worst belief about their relationship. He considered himself the same as the multitude of men who lusted after Meggie O'Day. But she wasn't Meggie; inside she was Megan, and she'd hoped Alex, at least, could tell the difference.

"Just keep away from me," she muttered and turned again to the fire.

* * *

Women.

Alex stacked an armload of wood near the fireplace and headed outside for more, not even glancing at Megan, curled under the covers on the single bed in the cabin.

If he never saw another one, it would be too soon.

They'd been snowbound for three days. They had been the worst three days of his life. She had barely been civil to him, more often than not spitting out sarcastic retorts to his every attempt at conversation. Try as he might, he couldn't understand what he'd done to infuriate her. He'd wanted her and said so. What was so wrong in that? He'd had his share of women during his time with the mounted police, and none had ever complained of his technique. He had never had the time or the inclination to get involved beyond the satisfying of physical needs. His mind had been focused on his career to the exclusion of all else; and then when he lost Joanna, he had added the burden of finding her killer. Those goals left little within him to give to another person.

The tension in the cabin remained as thick as the snow outside, made worse by his unwavering attraction to Megan regardless of her distaste for him. Right now, even though he stood outside without his coat in freezing temperatures, he grew warm and hard thinking of her under the covers in nothing but her underclothes.

He had been too long without a woman. That

was the problem. The Mounties were not allowed to avail themselves of the prostitutes on Paradise Alley. If he just spent a day in bed with a willing woman, his inconvenient need for Megan Daily would become a thing of the past.

The voice of conscience told him what he felt for her was beyond the physical. He had never felt such a desire to be with a woman, talk with her, know her in more ways than just her body. With Megan he felt complete, as though he'd come home. And God help him, he didn't care anymore how many men she'd had before him, as long as he was the last. But in her present mood, he doubted she would be receptive to those revelations.

Alex glanced up at the sky. The snow had stopped and the clouds drifted apart to reveal the long-absent sun. They could leave for Dawson City today. *Thank God.* One more day in such close quarters with Megan and he might break down and beg her to forgive him for whatever he'd done—anything, if only she'd smile at him, talk to him as if he were a human being and not a river rat, let him touch her silky hair and feast on her full lips.

A stray log fell from the pile in his arms and landed sharply on his toe. Alex winced, then sighed. It was no more than he deserved for letting his thoughts drift off course again.

He purposely let the armful of logs fall on the floor with a crash. Megan jumped up, startled from sleep. The blanket fell away, and Alex was treated to a glimpse of bare shoulders above her chemise before she snatched the cloth back to her neck.

"What's wrong?" she asked, blinking the sleep from her eyes.

"The snow stopped. I think we can leave this morning for town."

"Thank God."

Alex grimaced at the relief in her voice. "Pack up," he said gruffly and left to tend the horses.

When he returned, she had dressed and straightened the cabin. Her picnic basket and his saddlebags were packed and sitting by the door.

"Before we go, Lieutenant," Megan ventured, keeping with the formal manner of address she'd adopted during their time in the cabin. "I found something that might interest you in regard to my father and Willie Shore." She held out a charred piece of paper.

Taking it from her, he brushed her fingers with his and ignored her soft gasp of response. He quickly read the cryptic note and glanced at her. "When did you find this?"

"The first day, before you came. It was lying in the fireplace."

"You're just telling me now?"

She shrugged. "I thought you should know. What would you have done about it while we were stuck here?"

True, but he didn't like the fact that she'd kept the note from him. "I'm heartily sick of Willie Shore."

"Me, too," Megan agreed. "What do you make of that note?"

"Looks as though your father may have gone to meet Willie on the pass. I wish we could find this character. Might shed some light on both our problems."

"What does Willie have to do with your sister?"

Alex quickly filled her in on Geraldine's news.

"And you're just telling me this now?" she asked with a small smile.

Alex shrugged. "I wasn't sure what to make of the connection."

Megan walked slowly across the room to sit at the table. "Your sister knew Willie; my father knew your sister; Willie was my father's partner, and Willie asked my father to meet him on the day of his death, which was shortly before Joanna's suicide. Where does this leave us?"

"Looking for Willie Shore. Unless he died in that avalanche with your father, and there's really no way of knowing for sure. We've got to find him and make him tell us what he knows."

Megan stood. "The only way to do that is to get back to Dawson City. Shall we, Lieutenant?"

Alex nodded and followed her into the brisk Yukon air. The trip back was a silent one, the two of them preoccupied with their own thoughts and with guiding their horses through the snow.

When they reached the city, people were out and about as always. Very little kept the folk of Dawson inside for long. If they allowed themselves to be daunted by the snow and the cold and the darkness, they might as well go home.

Alex insisted on leaving Megan at the door to The Celebration and returning her horse to the stables himself.

"Honestly, Lieutenant, I can do for myself," she said, even as he helped her from the horse.

"I'm learning that." He put his hands to her waist, lifted. She slid down his body; and despite the heavy layers of clothing they wore against the elements, he swore he could feel every inch of her flesh sliding against his. He caught her lemon scent above the stinging freshness of the air and the teaming stench of the bodies and animals of Front street.

Because he wanted to hold on, he let go. Because he wished to pull her to him, he stepped back. Because he wanted nothing more than to be with her, he tipped his hat and said, "Good day."

Megan dressed slowly for work that evening, all the while thinking of Alex Carson. The strange longing on his face when he'd left her that afternoon haunted her still. She felt it, too.

She finished dressing and stepped out from behind the curtain only to discover Queen lounging on the bed.

Queen laughed at the shock on her face; and at her high-pitched cackle, Damon growled low and slunk from the room.

"Sorry," Megan apologized. "He just doesn't seem to take to you."

"Don't worry your head about it. I don't much care for him neither." She peered at Megan and sat up. "Your Mountie comin' tonight?"

"No. I don't think so." Megan shook her head. "He's not my Mountie."

"Sure he is. The lieutenant's lost his heart to you. Everyone can see that."

"I don't."

"You've got a lot to learn about men. That Mountie can't keep his eyes off you."

"He wants me. I know that. But I need more, Queen. I've seen too many women settle for less than they deserve and suffer for it. I won't let that happen to me."

"You talkin' about love and marriage and forever after?"

Megan sighed. "I don't know." She turned and stared up at the picture of her mother. "Mama and Papa were happy."

"Good luck, Lovey. I'm afraid you're talkin' to the wrong person about happy endings. I've seen a lot in my time here. In my opinion men are good for some laughs; then give 'em the boot before they break your heart."

"Maybe that would be best. Well, it doesn't matter anyway. Alex said he wants things to be strictly business between us from now on."

Queen gaped. "And you believed him? That man's got it for you bad. He might say he wants to cool things off, but I wouldn't be countin' on it if I were you. Make up your mind. If you want him, take him. If not, then maybe you should get out of town before you do get your heart busted."

"Get out of town?" Megan cried. "I'm not leaving. Not now, not ever. My father left me this place and the claim. They're the only things he ever gave me, and I won't give them up."

"Why don't you just sell that land and forget it. Mining's not proper for someone like you. Hell, most of the claims don't pan out anyhow."

"No, Queen. I plan to find out why my father filed a claim in the first place. He always insisted he would never be lured by gold in that way. He must have had a good reason to break his rule, and I won't rest until I catch up with Willie."

"Has the lieutenant been helpin' you with this?"

"Now that you mention it, yes." Megan was amazed to admit the fact even to herself. "If it hadn't been for Alex, I probably would have let the gold claim rest. I might have even gone back to San Francisco if he hadn't goaded me into staying by insisting I couldn't do it."

Queen didn't answer at first, appearing deep in thought. Then she heaved herself to her feet. "Well, Lovey, I admire a woman who knows her mind. You planning' on attendin' the dance to welcome Colonel Steele tomorrow night?"

"I haven't heard anything about it."

"Some of the merchant's have put together a dance to welcome the new Mountie commander. I'm surprised the lieutenant didn't mention it."

"Me, too," Megan muttered.

If that omission didn't confirm Alex's opinion

of her, nothing would. He was happy to stay with her in a deserted cabin and eager to share her bed, but he wouldn't be seen with her at a public function.

"Everyone in town will be there," Queen wheedled. "It won't do for Meggie O'Day to sit in her room all night."

"I suppose not." Megan sighed. "All right, I'll go. But only for an hour."

Queen gave a nod of approval. "See you downstairs." With a flick of her red nails, she disappeared through the doorway.

Alex frowned into the mirror as he combed his hair in preparation for the dance that evening. Though he had attempted to demur, his commander had made it clear Alex's attendance was mandatory. But he was in no mood for socializing. He had spent what little free time he had that day looking for Ian. The man's insinuations about Joanna had haunted Alex day and night since he had last seen Ian on the day of the sled dog race. But Ian was missing again, and no one in any of his businesses knew where he'd gone. Or if they knew, they were too frightened to tell Alex anything. He had finally given up when several of Ian's bodyguards, as if the man needed any, had started to follow him from door to door. He knew when retreat was the greater part of valor.

As he walked toward the large barn that had been cleaned and cleared for the dance, Alex wondered if Megan would be at the party. He was sure

Meggie O'Day would see the necessity of an appearance even if Megan Daily didn't want to attend.

Alex stepped inside to find the crowd thick and the music loud. It didn't take him long to locate Megan. The dress she wore, though cut low and suggestive, was a darker green than she usually favored, but Alex liked the way the color brought out the red fire in her hair.

Someone shoved a glass of punch into his hand, and Alex took a sip of the liquid as he moved closer to Megan. He grimaced at the bitter taste and dumped the contents onto the dirt at his feet. Looking up to see who had given him the horrid brew, he caught a furtive movement at the edge of his vision and watched as Ian McMurphy slipped outside. Alex hesitated, torn between the urge to follow the man he'd been searching for and the need to remove Megan from the attentions of other men.

He looked at her and at that moment Megan glanced up and her eyes met his. For just a moment, he saw a flash of confusion, the same confusion he'd witnessed in a doe he'd come upon drinking from a creek. Should I flee or should I fight, her eyes said before the shutters came down and she smiled at him too brightly. "Lieutenant, would you care to join us?"

Alex clenched his teeth at the false cheerfulness of her tone. "No." He stepped through the throng to clasp her hand and pull her to her feet. "I would care for you to join me." With a nod to the others, he pulled Megan with him onto the dance floor.

"You know I can't dance." She stumbled against him.

"There are too many people on the floor to dance. Just sway with the music and you'll be fine."

She resisted him for another second before relaxing in his arms and moving her feet in time with the waltz.

"Very good," he whispered in her ear and she stiffened again. "Relax," he soothed, running his palm up and down her tense back. "I won't hurt you."

"Quit doing that or I'll hurt you." The pointed heel of her shoe came down suspiciously close to his toe.

Alex smiled but stopped the movement of his hand, allowing his fingers to rest intimately on the curve of her hip. Megan glanced at him with a frown, but he met her gaze with an innocent expression and she merely narrowed her eyes and looked away.

"I thought we were going to stay away from each other," Megan said.

"No, we were going to keep things more businesslike between us," Alex corrected.

"I don't call dancing together business."

"But, Meggie, dancing is your business."

"Not mine," she grumbled, though she continued to dance.

He didn't know what had possessed him to ask her to dance, but now that they were on the floor, he felt better than he had all day. She fit so well against him, the top of her head just touching his chin. If he wanted, he could lean forward and rest his cheek against her hair, pull her head into the crook of his shoulder, and feel her breath upon his neck. His body responded to the fantasy and he missed a step.

"I thought you knew how to dance," Megan said.

"It's too crowded in here." He pulled Megan from the whirl of dancers and into a small, deserted tack room he'd seen on his way in.

"What do you think you're doing?" she demanded as he shut the door behind them.

"Getting away from the crush."

"I don't want to get away, especially with you. People are already talking about us. What do you think it will do for my reputation to be seen going into a room with you and shutting the door?"

"What reputation is that? The reputation of Meggie O'Day? I would think being involved with me would do wonders for your image. Queen seems to think so."

"Queen?" Megan paused in her agitated pacing. "What does Queen have to do with anything."

"She thinks being alone with me would do wonders for her reputation. I'm surprised you don't agree."

"When were you alone with Queen?"

Alex laughed and crossed the room. Megan went very still and looked up into his eyes. Alex couldn't resist. He reached out and caressed her too-pale cheek.

"Jealous?" he whispered and kissed her.

His mistake. With his body still hard and aching from their dance, the kiss only served to heighten the painful pleasure; and when Megan wound her arms around his neck, pressing her body against him to kiss him back, Alex groaned.

Megan pulled away. "Did I hurt you?"

Alex's lips tightened. "Oh, yes. You hurt me." He pulled her back into his embrace. "Do it again."

He caught a glimpse of her puzzled face before he resumed their embrace. He was constantly amazed at her show of innocence in matters between men and women. Maybe that was part of his attraction to her. The combination of the seductive allure of her body and the virginal innocence on her face. Alex pulled away and put his forehead to Megan's, breathing heavily.

"What's wrong?" she whispered, a slight hoarseness to her voice that made Alex smile despite the tension in his body.

"We've got to stop now or I won't be responsible for what comes next. I want you, Megan, but not on the dirt floor of a barn with hundreds of people beyond the door. You mean more to me than that."

At his words Megan pulled sharply away, as though she, too, had forgotten where they were. A blush tinted her cheeks and he marveled again at her shyness. How he wanted her! More than he had ever wanted any woman in his life.

"I'll take you back now." He winced at the stiffness in his voice.

Megan looked at him, and the hurt on her face told him she'd heard it, too. Well, perhaps that was for the best. Where she was concerned, his much lauded self-control became nonexistent.

"No need. I can see myself out, Lieutenant." Her emphasis on his rank gave the word the connotation of a curse.

With a swish of green satin, Megan rejoined the party. Alex remained alone in the cold room until he regained his control.

When he returned to the main room, a quick glance revealed Megan's absence. He moved to stand at the outskirts of the dance floor, watching the dancers for a few minutes. The novelty soon wore thin.

As he pushed through the crowd, planning to say his goodbyes to the colonel, the music suddenly seemed to pulse inside his head and breathing became difficult. He craved the cool air outside, but the doorway was too far away. His feet became heavier and heavier and the room shifted in front of his eyes. A woman screamed and Alex wondered what was the matter; then all thought ceased as blackness swallowed him and he fell into oblivion.

Megan watched in horror as Alex swayed then fell to the floor at her feet. She fell to her knees, reaching out a shaking hand to touch his forehead. He was so hot. Or was she too cold? Megan looked up at the sea of faces around her and focused on two Mounties.

"Take him to The Celebration," she ordered.

Colonel Steele stepped forward. "Who are you, miss?"

"Megan Daily, owner of The Celebration. I have a room where the lieutenant can rest alone and a doctor on my staff."

"I think he belongs at our headquarters. Perhaps your doctor can come there."

"I'm not wasting my time arguing with you, Colonel. This man needs attention, and I plan to see that he gets it as quickly as possible." Megan motioned to the Mounties, who hesitated, their eyes drifting to their commander.

"Very well," Colonel Steele conceded. "But I want to be kept up-to-date as to his condition."

Megan nodded, her gaze fixed on Alex's still, white face. She followed the men, hovering near Alex as they carried him through the streets of Dawson City and upstairs to a room near her own.

"Get Dan," she told Zechariah when he came to the door.

Minutes later the doctor appeared in the room but hesitated just inside the doorway. "Meggie, I'm not licensed to practice here." He shuffled his feet. "That's why I'm bartending."

"I don't care about your license, Dan. You've got the training; I want you to use it. I need someone I trust to take care of him."

With a deep breath, Dan squared his shoulders and came to stand at the bedside. "I have to examine him, Meggie. You'd best wait outside."

"No," Megan said, her eyes focused on Alex's face. "I won't leave him."

She set her chin, meaning to fight before she allowed him to remove her from Alex's side. Dan must have seen her determination for he said nothing more, quietly going about his examination.

"He's having trouble breathing, and his heart is beating too slow and irregularly. What exactly did he do before he passed out?"

"He was walking toward me. Then, suddenly, he staggered and fell. I was with him most of the time he was at the dance and he was fine."

"Did you see him eat or drink anything?" Megan wrinkled her brow, thinking back to when she'd first seen him. "He had a cup from the punch bowl in his hand, but it was empty."

Dan stood up and motioned for Megan to join him in the hall. She did so with an uneasy glance back at Alex. She didn't like leaving him, but he lay on the bed with no knowledge of her or anything else. Megan swallowed the fear rising in her throat.

"What's wrong with him?" she asked as soon as Dan shut the door behind them.

"I can't be sure. But I think he's been poisoned."

"Poisoned!" Megan cried. "But how? Why?"

"The most important question right now is, what? If I don't know what he was given, there's nothing I can do for him." Dan took her hand and Meggie felt cold, slick dread settle in her stomach. "Without that knowledge, Lieutenant Carson could well be dead by morning."

THIRTEEN

Megan listened as The Celebration went into full swing below her. The dance had ended an hour ago and many of the miners had returned to her place to continue the party. She sat in a chair next to the bed and watched over Alex.

Immediately after Dan's diagnosis she had sent word to Colonel Steele of Alex's condition and its probable cause. The commander had stopped in to inform her that no one else had fallen ill and so he believed the punch bowl was not contaminated in any way. None of Alex's fellow Mountie's had seen him eat or drink anything in their presence. Colonel Steele left, shoulders bent, and Megan knew he despaired of his lieutenant's life.

After doing what he could to make Alex comfortable, Dan retreated downstairs to serve drinks, cautioning Megan to call him if there were any change. So far, Alex continued to lie as still as death, his breathing harsh and irregular. The hand she held so tightly grew steadily colder, despite her efforts to warm it.

Standing up, Megan paced the room. She felt

so helpless. One minute Alex had been kissing her, insulting her, making her want him with a passion she had never thought possible. The next he lay still and cold, and she cursed herself for leaving him, for not taking advantage of the intense feelings he aroused in her. Now she might never have the chance.

A muffled groan from the bed had her whirling around and running to Alex's side. She went down on her knees and studied his face. *Had his color improved?*

She tilted her head, studying him more closely. She couldn't tell for sure, but she thought he might look a bit better. His chest still rose and fell with labored movements, but the breaths he took seemed more even. She would wait awhile before calling Dan.

Taking Alex's hand again, Megan laid her cheek against it and closed her eyes.

He knew he had to be dreaming because Joanna was alive.

Alex frowned and shifted, attempting to wake up. But a heavy weight pressed on his chest and his eyelids were too heavy to lift. Reality wavered, waned, and he slipped back into the dream.

"Alex, you made it home for my birthday." Joanna shrieked with glee as she launched herself into his arms.

Alex laughed, catching her around the waist and twirling her in a circle until they were both breathless and dizzy. "You should know, little sister, that

I would never miss your birthday on peril of death. Wait until you see what I've brought you."

"What? What?" She jumped up and down like a child anticipating a treat instead of the seventeen-year-old young woman she had become in his absence.

"Come now. You know you can't have your present until after supper."

"Alex, you always give me your present first. Don't tease."

He smiled at her, marveling at how beautiful she'd grown. They had always been close, and even his long absences with the mounted police had not dimmed their attachment. He had loved her from the day she was born, the little sister he had pledged to protect in his five-year-old exuberance. He had never broken that pledge. Please God, he never would.

"All right. You know I can't resist you when you smile like that." Alex drew a long, thin box from the pocket of his red uniform jacket. "I had this made especially for you."

With a gasp of delight, Joanna flipped the lid from the box and her mouth widened into a tiny "o" of surprise. She glanced up at him, her eyes incredibly blue in her heart shaped face.

"Alex. My first grown-up necklace. I love it."

She pulled the necklace from the box and held it up to the light. A small rose, struck in gold, hung from the center.

"It's perfect," she breathed and hastily fastened the gift around her neck.

"Glad you like it. Now that you're a lady, I thought you should have some women's things."

"Alex," Joanna threw her arms around his neck and kissed him soundly on the cheek. "You're the best brother a girl ever had."

Ever had . . . ever had . . .

The words echoed in his head, growing louder with each repetition until Alex groaned with the pain. Only a dream. Joanna was dead. Dead by her own hand. And he would never see her again in this life.

If only he had come home immediately when he received the letter from Joanna. He could still remember the pleading tone—which he had ignored.

Alex, please, please come home. Mama and Papa have never understood me, or my dreams. But you do. You said you'd always be there for me, and I need you now. I'll have to leave soon. I can't bear to stay here and be auctioned off like a prize cow. I'll have to run away.

Joanna's desire to become a singer had been sudden, unexpected and completely out of character, making Alex believe she was going through a phase of difficulty common to young women. A tiny rebellion before settling into marriage and family as she should. So, instead of going home as she'd asked, he'd fired off a chastising letter and gone on with his assignment in a remote part of the Canadian wilderness. By the time he had reached home, Joanna was gone as promised, and he had spent the next year searching for her—only to find her dead and buried in Dawson City. He would never forgive himself for not returning when she needed him.

"Alex."

The voice was familiar, feminine. Alex squinted and saw a bright light ahead. A figure awaited him; a voice called.

Joanna. But if Joanna were ahead of him and she were dead, then what did that make him?

"Alex!" He turned. Another voice called—feminine, urgent. He knew that voice.

Megan.

The path to her was dark. He could see nothing, but he heard her clearly. She was crying. He risked another glance toward the light. It was so soft and peaceful, so inviting. His sister beckoned.

He heard the sobs behind him and, with a sigh, turned away from the light. Pushing forward, he stumbled along the darkened path.

Alex opened his eyes. Light flared above him as music blared below. He was so tired and weak. He couldn't seem to lift his hand.

Glancing to the side, he saw that Megan slept with his hand clasped in hers. Tears streaked her cheeks. He frowned.

He had thought the sound of her crying a part of his dream. Had the dream been real then? What about the light and Joanna?

Alex reached over with his free hand and stroked Megan's damp cheek. She stirred, then bolted awake, her startled gaze flying to his face.

"Alex?" she whispered. "Oh, thank God."

"Why are you crying?" he asked, stroking his knuckles down her fine-boned jaw.

"I thought you were going to die. You collapsed at the dance, and then Dan said you were poisoned. Alex, you scared me to death." Megan got to her feet and drew a chair closer to the bed before sitting in it.

"I'm sorry. I can't remember anything after you left the dance." He frowned, striving to recall what had happened. "Poisoned, you say?"

"We don't know how or what or why. Do you have any ideas?"

"I came to the dance and someone gave me a cup of punch. I took a sip; but it was so bitter, I threw the rest out."

"I had some of the punch and it was too sweet, if anything. Who gave it to you?"

"I didn't notice." He looked into her eyes. "I was too busy staring at you. Then, when I tasted how awful it was, I looked around . . ." He paused, a stray memory dancing at the edge of awareness. "I saw someone and I wanted to go after him. But then I came to you instead."

"Who?" Megan leaned forward.

"I can't remember."

Alex's vision blurred and there were two Megan's, then one, then two again. He sighed and gave in as his eyelids became too heavy to keep open. As he drifted into sleep, he heard Megan shouting for Dan.

The next time he awoke, the room was dark, but a presence waited nearby. He shifted then moaned as pain shot behind his eyes. Immediately, Megan materialized next to his bed. "How do you feel?"

"Like I had a run in with a bottle of whiskey and my head lost."

"Would you like some water?" At his nod, she held a glass to his lips.

"How long have I been asleep?"

Megan sat on the edge of his bed. She wore a virginal white gown buttoned up to her neck. For some odd reason, the contrast excited him. Her hip brushed his thigh, and he gritted his teeth. He may have been half-dead for a while, but he was definitely alive now, as his body was making him painfully aware.

"You slept through the rest of last night and the morning. It's afternoon now. Everyone's asleep."

"Everyone but us." He took her hand.

Megan's eyes darted to his, unsure, a bit frightened. He smiled reassuringly, and she returned the smile, squeezing his hand as though he were a sick child.

"Dan said you'd be all right now. He figures that you only took in enough of the poison to make you ill but not enough to kill you. Colonel Steele is questioning everyone at the dance. So far, he's discovered nothing. Have you remembered who you saw after you were given the drink?"

"Hmm?" Alex had been studying her lips, enjoying the way they formed words as her teeth and tongue made rapid appearances and disappearances. "Ah, let me think." He concentrated, remembering the dance, Megan's laugh, the bitter taste of the punch, and his glance around the crowded room. "Damn. Ian." He sat up, his hand going to his head at the sudden movement. "I should have known. Who else would have the gall to poison a Mountie?"

"Ian? Are you sure? He hasn't been seen in town for several weeks."

"I'm sure."

Megan stood. "I'd better send word to Colonel Steele."

Alex grabbed her hand and pulled her back down next to him. "Not yet," he said and kissed her.

As his lips moved over hers, she gave in to the embrace and, after an initial resistance, melted against him, her hands caressing his bare chest.

He opened the top buttons of her nightgown and slipped his hands inside, running his fingertips down her long, smooth neck. Megan moaned into his mouth and deepened their kiss. She was all softness and womanly flesh as his hands roamed over her back and shoulders. No corsets or bustles inhibited his exploration as they had in the past. Though his head pounded in reaction to his ordeal, his body throbbed with need for her.

"No, Alex." Megan tore herself from his grip and moved out of his reach, her fingers unconsciously touching her mouth, then quickly rebuttoning the buttons he had just undone. "You nearly died and now . . . We can't."

"I didn't die, Megan. I'm very much alive as I'll show you if you come back here."

"No. I'm going to send a message to Colonel Steele and then have Dan look at you again."

"I don't want Dan looking at me. I want you."

"You may think you're strong enough, but you're not. I won't be party to making you ill." She turned and went to the door.

"You can run away if you want. But we both know what's between us is too strong to ignore. Next time we kiss, you won't be able to put off the inevitable. I'll make sure you won't want to."

Megan paused, and for a moment Alex thought she might return to his bed. Instead, she opened the door and disappeared into the darkened hallway without a word.

Megan had succeeded in avoiding Alex for a week, but the confrontation between them was long past due. His strength had returned, and he would be moving back to the barracks tomorrow. Then he planned to join the hunt for Ian McMurphy, which had gone on in his absence. The mounted police had scoured the town and surrounding area and had plans to carry the search further afield on the morrow.

As Megan climbed the stairs to her room, the exhaustion that had weighted her for the last week became even more pronounced. She had worked herself doubly hard in an attempt to gain the relief of sleep when she reached her room. But every night she lay awake, remembering the times Alex had kissed her, touched her, whispered her name, passion making the slight lilt of England in his voice all the more pronounced. After so many nights of those memories, the tension inside her was at an almost unbearable level.

She reached the top of the staircase and opened the door to her room. Stepping inside, she locked it behind her. Without bothering to turn on the lights she disrobed, then put on her dressing gown. As she fastened the row of tiny white buttons up the gown's front she walked across the room to her bed.

"Working hard this week?"

Megan shrieked and jumped away from the bed as a voice came from the darkness. Hurrying across the room, she turned on the lights and stared at Alex Carson reclining on her bed in nothing but his black pants. Damon lay at his feet, blinking in confusion at the sudden light in his eyes. After fixing an annoyed yellow glare upon her, the wolf jumped from the bed and went to curl up behind her dressing screen.

"What are you doing here?" Megan hissed.

"You might have been able to avoid me all week, but not anymore."

"Avoid you? Why would I do that? I've been working."

"I'm sure you have. But now The Celebration is closed and it's just you and me."

Alex stood and crossed the room to stand before her. "If you really want me to leave," he said softly and pulled the pins from her hair, one by one, "I will."

Her elaborate hairstyle collapsed like a tent in the midst of a storm, and Megan's hair tumbled around her shoulders. She looked into Alex's blue eyes. She wanted him in her room and in her bed more than she'd wanted anything in her life. With a sigh of surrender, she tilted her lips to meet his.

They had kissed before, but never with the knowledge that they would soon be as one. That knowledge added a hunger to their embrace that soon had her moaning with need. No man had ever affected her in this way, and she wondered briefly what her life would have been like if one had. She had always been able to remain aloof before because her emotions had never been involved. That time was past.

He pressed her back against the door, his lips traveling over her face then down to her neck. As he nipped her sensitive flesh, his broad, callused fingers learned the curves and valleys of her breasts through the fabric of her nightdress. His thumbs teased her hardened nipples then his head dipped, and he captured one bud and drew it into his mouth, the stroke of his tongue through the cotton adding an extra dimension of sensation. Her hands grabbed for his shoulders as her knees threatened to buckle.

He moved closer, his body pinning hers against the cold wood, and she walked her fingers over his shoulders and down his back, testing and pressing against the solid muscle and bone as he turned his attentions to her other nipple. She could feel the part of him that pulsed with life pressing at the juncture of her thighs, and her hips moved of their own volition to press against him.

At the movement, he gasped her name, and his hands went to the buttons of her gown. He fumbled there for a moment before cursing, then rending the material in two to expose her nakedness. The cool air on her heated flesh made her shiver. He lifted her into his arms as he had once before in that very room, but this time there would be no interruptions.

He placed her on the bed and lay next to her on his side, one arm supporting his head. She watched his face as he examined her, his fingers trailing the path of his eyes. He caressed her neck, a finger outlining the path of her collarbone and then dipping into the valley between her breasts. He continued downward, fingers splaying across her belly and then tangling in the red curls below. She arched as a finger touched the bud of her womanhood, then entered. Stroking, probing until she bit her lip to keep from screaming.

"Do you like that?" His breath caressed her cheek.

She nodded, eyes closed, and bit back a guttural moan as his lips and teeth pulled at her breast, harder and more urgent than before.

"I've wanted this from the first moment I saw you. Tell me you want me, too."

"You know I do." She gasped as his fingers teased and his mouth promised.

"Tell me."

Somehow he removed his pants, and his burning arousal pressed against her thigh. She should have been frightened; instead, she felt bold and reached down to grasp him in her hand, surprised at the heat and the strength she found there.

Opening her eyes, she met his hooded gaze. "I want you, Alex."

He moved above her, rubbing his shaft against her swollen core, prolonging the moment until her hands grasped at his buttocks, silently pleading with him to end the torment. With the whisper of her name on his lips, he entered her.

His face clouded with confusion when he encountered her innocence and he froze. Frightened he might withdraw and end the exquisite sensations she was just beginning to understand, she arched against him and the thin membrane broke. Her gasp of pain was swallowed as his lips devoured hers, and soon pleasure overrode every other sensation as they strained together toward their ultimate goal.

He stiffened, then plunged into her a final time. At the movement, the tension that had built inside her since the first time he had kissed her crested, then broke and shattered within her.

When they were still and their breathing had slowed, he shifted to the side and glanced down at the bed beneath them. She followed his gaze and saw the telltale mark of blood. She met his puzzled gaze.

"Why didn't you tell me? I would have been more gentle."

"I did tell you." She pulled the covers over her nakedness, suddenly feeling exposed. "You refused to believe me."

"What was I supposed to think, Megan? The way you dress, the life you've led, this place. You've got to be the last virgin in the Yukon."

"Not anymore," she said quietly.

"No. I'm sorry."

Her gaze flew up to meet his and she could see that he was, indeed, sorry. Her heart ached. She had given him an incredible gift, and his only re-action was regret. A sudden anger filled her. "Get out."

"What?"

"You heard me. Get out."

"Why?" he asked, but he was already picking up his pants.

"This is my room and my place. I don't have to explain myself. Just get out."

With a last confused look over his shoulder, Alex left the room. Megan picked up a glass from her bedside table and heaved it at the door.

The thump against the door was followed by the shattering of glass. Alex hesitated, wondering if he should go back in and make her explain herself. The sound of another glass breaking made up his mind. He would talk to her tomorrow.

How was he to have known she was a virgin? Sure, she'd said she was no whore, but that didn't mean she was untouched. He felt guilty for having been so rough with her when it was her first time, although she hadn't complained and he could swear she'd enjoyed herself as much as he had.

"Late night, Lieutenant?"

Alex looked up to see Queen lounging in the doorway to her room. She smirked. She must have seen him leave Megan's room. In his nearly un-clothed state, it was obvious what he'd been doing there.

"Shouldn't you be asleep?"

"Too much noise out here." She glanced behind him toward Megan's room as another thump and shatter resounded from inside. "Never thought our Meggie had such a temper. What'd you do? Go too fast for the girl?"

"Shut up, Queen. I'm not in the mood," Alex said and entered his own room, closing the door to prevent any further discussion.

Nevertheless, Queen's high-pitched cackle came to him loud and clear.

FOURTEEN

Three weeks passed and Alex avoided The Celebration. He hoped, given enough time, Megan would allow him to apologize without throwing something at him. After going over their encounter in his mind, he realized his shock over her virginity had hurt her. She had given him a gift no other could ever possess. She had trusted him with herself, and he had not trusted her word. He had spent much of his time in the last few weeks berating himself for his stupidity and trying to think of a way to get her to forgive him.

The day was cold and dark, typical for October in the Yukon. Alex walked down the street, nodding to those he passed, though it was hard to tell who anyone was amidst the muffle of their coats and hats. No sign of Ian McMurphy had been found, though guards were posted at his home and major places of business.

Alex stopped. His steps had led him to The Celebration. Well, maybe now was as good a time as any to confront Megan. She should be in her room resting for the evening to come. He entered the saloon.

"Hey, Lieutenant," Zechariah called from his room near the door. "If you're lookin' for Meggie, she ain't here."

Alex frowned. Just his luck. He'd come to make peace and she was off God knew where. "When will she be back?"

Zechariah scratched his head. "Don't rightly know. She took her wolf and said she was goin' for a walk. She usually goes out past the stables by the hill overlooking town. Crazy gal. Its too cold for that nonsense. Anyways, she didn't leave more than a few minutes ago. You can catch her."

Alex nodded and hurried out the door. It didn't take him long to locate Megan. He watched her walk up ahead, arms clasped around her sides for warmth. The wolf ran in front of her, pausing to sniff at points of interest then racing to catch up.

She looked sad, Alex thought, and knew he must be the cause. He quickened his steps, determined to put an end to their estrangement.

Megan bent to look at something along the path, and Damon trotted over to join her. At the same moment, a shot rang out and the wolf started with a yelp.

Alex sprinted the remaining distance between him and Megan, pulling her behind a rock and pushing her down beneath him as he drew his revolver.

Megan struggled, one of her elbows connecting to his midsection, and his breath whooshed out.

"Stay down," he croaked and peered around the rock.

Damon lay on the path, and Alex could see he still lived. The animal was attempting to crawl after Megan, leaving a trail of blood on the frozen ground. Alex scouted the surrounding area, but it was too dark to see very far. In fact, it was so dark, whoever had fired the shot must have been close.

"Do you see anyone?" Megan whispered.

"I think he's gone."

He fired a shot into the air, hoping to draw the assailant's fire, but no gunshot echoed his.

"Lieutenant? Meggie?" a voice called.

"Who's there?" Alex demanded.

"Dan." The doctor ran into view, stopping next to Damon. "I was at the stable and heard shots. You two all right?"

"We're fine; but as you can see, Damon needs your attention. I want you to take him and Megan back to The Celebration."

"Where are you going?" Megan asked as Alex helped her to her feet.

"I'm going after whoever's out there. There've been too many 'accidents' where you're concerned. If you hadn't bent down and Damon hadn't gotten in the way, I think you'd be the one on the ground right now. I don't plan to give him a second chance."

Grabbing her by the shoulders, he planted a hard kiss on her mouth. "We've got things to discuss when I get back, Megan, and you're going to listen to me."

He turned and headed into the wild countryside. Megan's voice followed him into the darkness. "Be careful, Alex."

He made good progress for the next hour. Luckily for him, the weather had been unseasonably warm the previous day, softening the top layer of snow. Clear footprints led away from town. Whoever he followed was big, judging by the size of the boots, and quick, since Alex moved fast but was unable to gain much ground. He was hindered by the fact that he had to pause in the darkness to check for the trail.

Over the next two hours he gained on his quarry. When he entered a cove of trees he recognized from previous visits to Brian Daily's claim, he proceeded cautiously. The trail led through the midst of the pines, and he followed, keeping a close watch for an ambush. He had nearly reached the end of the trees when the footprints in front of him suddenly stopped. Puzzled, he bent down and examined the ground, then peered around the area, eyes straining against the darkness. The pine trees surrounding him were merely shadows, and the slight wind that had sprung up whistled eerily through their branches.

He wasn't mistaken. The prints had stopped, as though the wearer of the boots had vanished into thin air.

Thin air? Aw hell. He looked up.

A dark figure leapt from the tree above and pain exploded in Alex's head before his world went black.

* * *

"Looks like he's going to be fine. We'll just have to try and get him to rest for a few days."

Megan heaved a sigh of relief at Dan's words and smoothed the coarse, black fur on Damon's head. When they had carried him back to the dance hall and up to her room, she had been horrified at the amount of blood soaking the fur of his shoulder. But after examination, Dan declared the bullet had only grazed the wolf, creating a cut in need of stitching but no permanent damage.

When Dan left, Megan began to shake. The thought of what might have happened if she had not bent down at that particular moment or if Damon had not come between her and the bullet terrified her. She wished Alex would return and bring the sense of safety his presence gave her. She longed for the warmth of his arms and the sound of his deep voice whispering into her hair that everything would be all right.

Evening came and she went to work, listening to her customers with half her attention, the other half focused on the door as she prayed for Alex's return. The night seemed endless as her nerves stretched to the breaking point. More than once she lost a hand of cards through inattention, and she ruined her dress when her unsteady fingers knocked a drink into her lap. She told herself he must have come back exhausted and gone straight to bed. He would come to her in the morning and then her night fears would be so much foolishness. But when morning came and he still had not arrived, she grabbed her coat and trudged through the snow to the offices of the mounted police.

There she learned he had not reported for duty and her fear increased. She informed the officer of what had occurred the previous afternoon and he sent a man in Alex's wake. Then there was nothing to do but return to The Celebration and wait as the cold dread settled deep in her soul.

Alex lay on the ground in the snow, trees blocking the dark sky above him. Because of the absence of the sun twenty-four-hours-a-day during the winter, he had no idea how long he had been unconscious. With a groan, Alex sat up and put a hand to his throbbing head. His fingers encountered a sticky substance at the temple—blood frozen to his skin. Grimacing, he forced himself to stand.

The world swayed and he gritted his teeth, fighting the weakness. He couldn't remain in the open where there was too much danger from exposure or wolves. He had to find shelter until he was stronger. He vaguely remembered being near the claim cabin and stumbled from the copse of trees. His feet and hands tingled, warning him he needed to get inside soon or risk frostbite.

He reached a hill and fell, climbing the rest of the incline on his hands and knees in the snow. When he reached the top he sighed in relief. Below lay the cabin and safety.

It seemed to take a long time to reach the building; and when he did, his face stung from the biting cold and he fumbled with the door, afraid he wouldn't be able to open it, his hands were so stiff. With a creak the portal gave way and Alex fell into the room.

As quickly as he could in his weakened state, he lit a lamp and built a fire, relishing the pain as the blood flowed back into his near frozen limbs. When his hands were in working order once again, he filled a pan with snow and heated it over the stove, then washed the blood from the cut on the side of his head. Once it was cleaned, he saw that the gash was not as bad as he'd feared and, though it might leave a scar, he should have no permanent damage.

He had to thank his guardian angel that whoever he had been following had not stayed around to finish him off. He must have assumed Alex would die of exposure before returning to consciousness.

Alex stumbled across the room to lie on the bed, knowing he needed to rest before attempting the return trip to Dawson City. By now, Megan had surely alerted the Mounties to his absence and one of his fellow officers was probably hot on his trail. Unless new snow obliterated the tracks, he would have assistance in returning to town.

He awoke several hours later feeling much stronger, minus the headache. The night was clear, no sign of a storm. He set about making a meal with the staples he had left on his last visit to the cabin. Before the soup was done, a young Mountie burst inside.

"Carson, you had better have a good explanation for leading me on such a chase in this weather."

"Sorry, Jackson," he told the recruit. "Whoever took a shot at Miss Daily got a jump on me and knocked me over the head."

"Someone got a jump on you? That's a new one. Think it was McMurphy?"

Alex frowned. "Could have been him. The person I saw was big enough to be McMurphy."

Alex glanced around the cabin. He knew from previous visits that someone had been living in the place on and off. Might that someone be Ian McMurphy? If so, then where was he now?

The two men sat down to eat before braving the return trip.

"Hey, Carson. Look what I found hanging outside. Does it belong to your lady friend?" Jackson held up a necklace.

The light from the lamp caught the gold and turned it to burnished amber. Alex's throat closed off and he stared, entranced, as the rose twirled round and round. Reaching out, he snatched the necklace from the surprised Mountie's hand.

"Where did you get this?" he rasped.

Jackson frowned, puzzled. "It was hanging from a hook right outside the door of this place. I noticed it when I walked up. Is it yours?"

Alex clenched Joanna's necklace in his fist and stood, walking away from the table to stare into the fire.

Joanna's necklace, here at Brian Daily's cabin. What did that mean? Had it been there all along and he'd never seen it? Had Joanna left it here herself or had it been left by the mysterious occupant? Was it Willie Shore who stayed in the cabin . . . or Ian . . . or someone else entirely?

He was sick to death of the questions. He wanted to know who had left his sister to die, who the mysterious Willie Shore was, and why the answers to those questions were so important that someone had tried to kill both him and Megan.

"Finish up," he said. "We're going back to Dawson City."

Megan was losing steadily at poker when Alex came through the door. Throwing her cards onto the table, she launched herself into his arms without thought and kissed him.

His lips were cold, but they warmed under hers and parted. Memories of their night together surfaced, and she melted into his embrace.

The cheers brought her around. Blushing, Megan pulled back and glanced around the room. Every man in the place grinned from ear to ear at her display. She took Alex's hand and led him through the dance hall and upstairs to her room. To hell with dignity, she wanted answers.

As soon as the door closed behind them, he tried to pull her back into his arms, but she resisted. "Alex, where have you been? Did you catch the person who shot at me?" She reached up and touched his face. "What on earth happened to your head?"

"I'm glad to see you're not angry anymore. Does

this mean you forgive me for my stupidity the last
time we were together?"

"I've been worried about you." She frowned.
"One thing doesn't have anything to do with the
other. I want to know what happened."

"I trailed the culprit to a copse of trees near
your cabin, where he jumped me from a tree and
knocked me over the head."

"Oh, no." Her lower lip trembled, and she bit
down on it, hard, to still the motion. "You could
have been killed."

"But I wasn't. And that fact alone has me wondering what's going on around here. The questions
we've been asking have led to attempts on both
our lives. We've got to find Willie Shore soon or
I'm afraid that the next attempt will be successful.
I need to talk to Queen."

"Queen? What for?"

"Ian's vanished, although the person I followed
was large enough to be him. Ian seems to be pretty
fond of Queen, and I thought she might be persuaded to tell me if he has a claim of his own or
a friend who does."

"You'd better let me talk to her."

Alex's forehead wrinkled in confusion. "Why?"

"You know how she is, Alex. She'll just make a
joke out of your questions. She doesn't trust law-
men. I might be able to convince her to tell me
something, woman-to-woman."

Alex hesitated, clearly uneasy at the thought of
letting her do what he considered his job. Finally,

he nodded. "All right. But I want to know exactly what she says as soon as you've talked to her."

"Fine, but I'd do best to wait until we close tonight. She wouldn't be too receptive to me if I cut into her dance time."

"True," he agreed, moving to the door. "I have to get back and talk to the colonel. I don't think you should leave The Celebration without me. I'll stop by later." He opened the door, then paused. "And Megan . . ."

"Yes?"

"Thanks for worrying about me." He leaned over and kissed her quickly on the lips before slipping out the door.

Megan crossed the room to sit at her desk. He hadn't exactly apologized for his behavior the night they'd made love. But he seemed to be sorry he hadn't trusted her. Still, she yearned for some acknowledgment of the fact that she'd given herself to him when she had never done so with any other. But to ask for the words would render the sentiments useless. Knowing the depth of Alex's commitment to his job and his sister, any relationship would be relegated to second place until he had the answers he craved. And what if the answer were that her father had, indeed, abandoned Joanna? Would Alex ever be able to look at her without seeing the daughter of the man who had driven Joanna Carson to her death? Would she be able to look at him without wondering if he thought just that?

By the time the dance hall was empty and

Megan went looking for Queen, the woman had already gone to her room. Climbing the stairs, Megan hoped fervently that her friend had not gone to bed yet. Tales of Queen's temper upon being awakened after a night of hard work were legend. Megan didn't need a tongue-lashing, but she had to talk to Queen—or Alex would.

She knocked tentatively on the door to the woman's room, letting out the breath she'd been holding when Queen called a jovial, "Come on in."

The dancer lounged on her bed in her favorite purple silk robe. Megan often wondered if Queen had to pay extra for her clothes since they obviously needed more material than usual for an average dress.

"Lovey, I thought you'd be sleepin' by now. Or at least entertainin' that man of yours."

Megan blushed, uncomfortable with the knowledge that everyone knew about her relationship with Alex.

"I wanted to talk to you." Megan pulled a chair next to the bed.

"There a problem downstairs?"

"Nothing like that. We're making money hand over fist here thanks to your help. I wonder that Papa never asked you to be a partner, Queen. You really have a talent for bringing in the customers."

"Brian asked, but I wasn't interested. I like to pick up and move on when the mood takes me. Brian understood that."

"You were good friends."

"We were at that. Never met a man I could get along with like your papa."

"What about Big Ian?" Megan asked, seeing her opening and jumping in with both feet.

Queen frowned. "What about him?"

"He seems to have taken a liking to you."

"So have a lot of others. That doesn't mean I want to marry 'em."

"No, I just wondered how well you knew Ian."

Queen's eyes narrowed, and Megan stifled the urge to squirm under her friend's gaze.

"What's it to you?" Queen asked.

"I wondered if he ever mentioned having a claim on the Bonanza or if he might go and visit someone who did?"

"Why?"

"He's been missing a long time and I thought maybe he'd gone to work a claim."

"Ian's got his finger in enough pies in town, he don't need to be mining a claim. Where'd you get such an idea?" Understanding dawned on Queen's face. "You're questioning me for your Mountie friend. They can't find Ian, so he sent you to see if I knew where the big ox might be holed up. Well, even if I did, I'm no liver-faced snitch."

"I know that." Megan attempted to soothe the woman, though she *had* hoped to get Queen to "snitch."

"Well, make sure you remember it then." Queen sniffed. "When you tell me somethin', you can rest assured I'll take it to my grave."

"Thanks, Queen. You've been a real friend."

Megan stood to leave and Queen rose as well. As she did, something fell from the pocket of her gown, hitting the floor with an odd sound. Megan bent to pick it up, her fingers closing around the hard object seconds before the dancer's. Megan rose and opened her hand.

Resting on her palm lay a nugget of gold worth a small fortune.

FIFTEEN

Queen snatched the nugget from Megan's hand and popped it down the front of her robe. "Thanks, Lovey, wouldn't want to lose that."

"I've never seen a nugget so big. Where'd you get it, Queen?"

"One of the boys gave it to me. You know how they're always begging me to run away with 'em. They try to bribe me, too. I've got lots of 'em, and I usually just spend 'em as fast as I get 'em, but this one was so purty I decided to hold onto it for a while. If them boys want to throw away their gold on me, I say let 'em. A girl's got to look out for her future." Queen tilted her chin as if daring Megan to argue with her.

"True," Megan agreed, wondering as she moved toward the door how many of the other girls had such caches in their rooms. "Sleep well, Queen."

"Sorry I couldn't tell you nothin' about Ian. Tell your Mountie that the big ox will turn up sometime. He just has to be patient."

Megan returned to her room and replaced her

work clothes with a dressing gown, taking down her elaborate hairstyle and twisting the heavy mass into a single braid. As she did so, she wandered around her rooms, coming to a stop in front of the painting of her mother.

The fire in the grate warmed her as she stared at the beloved picture. She had been toying with the idea of moving the painting into her bedroom where she could see it better. Deciding there was no time like the present, Megan moved a chair in front of the fireplace and climbed up, pulling the heavy painting from the wall and awkwardly getting down from her perch. When she glanced back at the now-empty wall, her mouth fell open in surprise. A small door with a lock had been built into the wall.

Climbing back onto the chair, Megan examined the door. There was no handle, only the small hole for a key would open the panel. But where was the key?

She glanced around the room, her brow furrowed with concentration. Where would Papa hide a key?

Her eyes lit on the bedside lamp and she heard her father's voice. "Meggie girl, I always put my valuables under the mattress. You know I'm a light sleeper. No one's going to get past me when I'm in dreamland."

Slowly, she climbed down from the chair and went to the bed, her hand searching beneath the mattress until her fingers encountered a small metal object. Withdrawing it, she looked down at the key in her palm, then glanced up at the locked door. What could be so important that Papa had locked it away? She hurried to find out.

A sharp knock froze her in place, and her gaze went to the door; thankfully, the lock she had ordered was now in place.

"Who's there?" she called.

"Alex. Can I come in?"

"I'll be right there."

Dropping the key into the pocket of her gown, Megan replaced the painting and returned the chair to its place; then she went to open the door. Damon slipped out, and she let him go, knowing Zechariah would allow the now-recovered wolf out to roam the night.

Alex stepped into the room and locked the door behind him before taking her into his arms. Megan had no time to protest before his lips came down on hers.

She had meant to tell him that what was between them could not continue. She couldn't be what he needed, didn't want to be the lieutenant's woman. But all her protests fled as his lips and hands worked their magic.

Somehow they ended up on the floor in front of the fireplace. The heat from the fire matched the heat growing within her, and it was a relief when her gown fell away and the fur rug softly caressed her back. Alex murmured against her warm skin, and she arched against him, welcoming him into her with a sigh.

Afterward, they lay entwined and she smoothed

his auburn hair back from his brow, then burrowed against his side. She had never felt more at home with another human being. Perhaps she should forget about what had happened to the other women she had known. She was strong, after all. She wouldn't fall apart if this man left her. She would always survive.

"Marry me, Megan," Alex whispered, and the words echoed in the room, soft next to the crackling of the fire.

"Excuse me?" she asked.

Alex propped himself up on an elbow and tangled his fingers in her hair, which had come loose from its braid.

"I want you to marry me. As soon as the ice breaks, I'll take you away from here. You'll never have to work in a place like this again. I'll make you happy, I swear."

He stared into her eyes with a desperation that confused her. Suddenly, understanding dawned. He was trying to save her. He had failed to save Joanna; so instead, he would save Meggie O'Day and absolve himself from his guilt over his sister.

"No, thank you," Megan said primly and pulled away from him.

"What?" Alex asked, shock evident in his voice.

"I said, 'No, thank you.' I'm perfectly happy in Dawson City. I like to work. You don't have to save me from myself, Alex."

"But, but . . . I want to marry you. You were a virgin. You gave yourself to me."

"I don't *give* myself to anyone, Lieutenant. I

slept with you and we both enjoyed ourselves. Let's leave it at that, shall we? I care for you, I admit. More than I've cared for any man beyond my father. But I don't need a man to survive. I never will."

She turned away and slipped on her dressing gown, her fingers going to the pocket to feel the key still resting there. She glanced up at the portrait of her mother. What lay hidden behind it?

Alex dressed silently, obviously confused that she hadn't fallen all over him with gratitude for his proposal. "I'll ask you again when you've had some time to think," he said.

"The answer will be the same, Lieutenant."

Alex stared at her for several moments, then shrugged. Megan could tell he thought she'd change her mind, and she gritted her teeth with irritation.

"Did you learn anything from Queen?" Alex asked.

She grasped at the change of subject. "I'm afraid not. She insists Ian is pursuing her and she wants nothing to do with him. She thinks he'll turn up eventually to check on his businesses."

"She's probably right, though I'd prefer to talk to him before one of us ends up dead."

A chill ran down Megan's spine and she turned away, her gaze again drawn to her mother's picture. Should she tell Alex about the secret door? Maybe an answer lay hidden there. No, she would keep the door to herself until she knew what was behind it. Brian must have had a good reason to build the door, and she would not betray his trust yet. If any answers came to light, she could then share the knowledge with Alex.

"I'm tired, Alex," she said, her eyes still on the picture.

He came up behind her and his hands rested on her shoulders. "Your mother?"

"Yes.

"She's lovely. You have the look of her."

"Thank you. She was very frail and gentle. Too much so for this world."

"You take after your father in spirit then." Alex turned her to face him. "You're a survivor. I admire that. But you don't have to prove it to me. It doesn't take away any of your strength to spend your life with another person; you only add that person's strength to your own."

Megan gazed into Alex's eyes and saw the warmth and strength of the man. He ran his knuckles gently down her cheek then kissed her brow before he took his leave.

She waited only a moment before locking the door and removing the portrait. The key in her pocket fit the lock, and the door opened with a slight creak. Inside lay a small book, which she removed carefully, then climbed down from the chair and went to sit on the bed.

The book was black and leather-bound with the look of a diary. She flipped open the cover and recognized her father's handwriting.

Meggie—Let no one see this book but you. If you are reading this, I am dead. Suffice it to say, I did not die

*by accident but by design. Read what I have recorded
herein and know that I have always loved you. Papa.*

Megan raised her head for a moment, tears
stinging even as uncertainty clouded her mind. He
had not died by accident? How could that be when
an avalanche was nothing if not an accident?
Reaching over, she turned up the lamp and read
on.

*While I was at the claim, someone shot at me. Willie
was with me and, after the intruder in my room the other
night, feels something is amiss. We returned to The Celebration together. I am lucky to have such a friend.*

Megan frowned. The attempts on her father's
life followed a similar pattern to the attempts on
the lives of both her and Alex. Either the killer
was not very original or not very bright.

She read the book from cover to cover, much
of it detailing Brian's trip up the Chilkoot Pass and
the beginnings of The Celebration. He later wrote
of the claim on Bonanza Creek and his hope that
the mine would bear fruit. Brian mentioned Willie
often, Joanna Carson not at all. If her father had
traveled with Joanna, created a child with her,
wouldn't he have mentioned the woman once in
his diary? Despite her father's admonition to keep
the book to herself, Megan knew she would show
it to Alex. It would bring him one step closer to
finding the man who had hurt Joanna if he knew
he no longer had to prove Brian Daily's culpability.

*I walk in fear of my life each day. If only I knew
whom to trust. Willie would profit most by my death,
especially if Megan leaves Dawson City without claiming*

the mine; but I have trusted my partner with my life before and I will not start doubting now. I feel the threat drawing nearer. If not for Damon watching my back, I would not leave my room.

The diary ended there, and Megan put the book aside as she stared into space. The final entry worried her. Why would someone want to kill her father? The Celebration had been left to Megan, as had his share in the mine. He had no enemies that he mentioned. Brian had always been everyone's friend. There was also the matter of the note she had found at the cabin, which had asked Brian to meet Willie at the base of the pass. But her father never mentioned such a note in his diary. And Brian had died in an avalanche, a chance occurrence if ever there was one; how could his death have been anything but an accident? Instead of answering her questions as she'd hoped, the diary only served to add more questions and cloud the answers she already had.

A knock on her door had her glancing at the clock next to her bed. Afternoon. Megan sighed and rubbed her tired eyes. She had read the diary when she should have been sleeping, and now she would have to get dressed in a few hours for work.

After pushing the diary under a pillow, Megan crossed the room and opened the door, moving aside as Damon streaked past her legs. Alex Carson stepped into the room, leaning against the door to shut it.

"Did you miss me?" He pulled her close.

"No . . . yes . . . I—" Megan stuttered.

"I thought so," he said and kissed her.

Megan pushed against his chest and tore her lips away before her traitorous body allowed a repeat performance of that morning's activities.

"I thought I told you I wouldn't marry you," she gasped.

"You did. However, you said nothing about sleeping with me."

Megan knew her mouth hung open in surprise. "You mean you still want to sleep with me even after I've said I won't marry you?"

"Of course. We haven't been married either of the times I made love to you." He pulled her back into his arms. "If you'd like to reconsider my offer, I'm thrilled. If not, well, we can continue on the way we have been."

"You still want to see me?"

"Of course. If I can't have you as my wife, I'm perfectly happy to be content with you as my mistress."

Mistress. Megan frowned. The word conjured up images of women in houses paid for by men, their clothes bought by men, the very food they ate provided at the whim of men. No, that was not what she wanted.

"I can take care of myself, Alex. I have no need of your protection."

"Fine. Then we'll just enjoy each other for as long as we . . . enjoy each other."

Megan stared at him for several seconds, pondering the offer. She had to admit she enjoyed him, she enjoyed what they did together. If that enjoyment were good enough for a man, why shouldn't it be the same for a woman?

"All right," she agreed. "As long as you understand that I will not be kept and I will not marry you."

Alex merely smiled and kissed her until she forgot what she had been saying. He carried her to the bed, and as he lay her back on the pillows, her head struck the diary and she paused.

"Alex, I have something to show you," she said.

"Good," he murmured against her skin.

"No, really." She reached under the pillow and pulled out the book. "My father's diary."

Alex froze, then lifted his head slowly until his gaze met hers. "You had his diary and you never told me?"

"I just found it last night, after you left." She pointed to the painting of her mother she had replaced in its original position to hide the door in the wall. "There's a safe hidden behind the portrait."

Alex sat up and took the book from her, flipping it open to the first page. After scanning the message there, he looked up briefly then moved to the desk and began to read.

An hour later, Alex tossed the book onto the desk and turned toward Megan as she waited in front of the fireplace. "He never mentions Joanna." No emotion graced his voice.

"I think that proves he isn't the man you're looking for."

"Or maybe she meant so little to him he didn't even bother to record her existence."

"I don't think so. He talks about Willie enough. I'm sure he would have written about Joanna if he were involved with her."

Alex nodded and joined her on the rug before the fire. "I agree. I've hated him for so long, and now to find out I was wrong . . . I don't know what to do next."

"The same thing we've been doing. Keep looking for Willie and Ian. The answers will fall into place eventually, Alex. But knowing what happened to Joanna and my father won't bring them back. We have to go on with our lives without them."

Alex took her hand, but continued to stare into the flames. "I can't regret searching for Brian since my search led me to you."

Megan smiled and leaned against him. "I'm glad, too. Though I must say you weren't too appealing in the beginning."

"And now?" Alex asked as he took her into his arms.

"Now, I find you irresistible."

Alex stood and drew Megan to her feet. "Show me," he said, as he led her to the bed.

She undressed him piece by piece, pausing to kiss and caress each inch of flesh revealed to her questing lips. His flesh was warm and smelled of fresh soap and man. She rubbed her cheek against the soft curls covering his chest and then flicked her tongue over the round, flat disc of a male nipple. When her fingers traced the hardened outline of him through his pants, Alex muttered an oath and moved away from her long enough to remove the rest of his clothing then he yanked the belt of her robe free, opening the garment and freeing her bare skin for his hands.

They tumbled back onto the bed, a mass of limbs and teeth and lips. He gathered her hair into his fists and held her still, staring into her eyes as though he wished a view into her soul. Then, whispering her name, he bent his head and his mouth plundered hers.

She opened her mouth and met his tongue with her own, allowing her hands to roam down the taut flesh of his torso before she clasped his buttocks to pull him closer.

His lips traveled from her mouth to her neck, where he nibbled for a moment before moving on to sweeter delights. His hands found her breasts, cupping them together as he bent his head to run a tongue over their distended tips. Megan arched, aching for more, and bit her lip to keep from crying out as Alex took a nipple into his mouth, biting it gently before laving the hurt with his tongue. Then he drew her into his mouth and suckled so slowly and deeply she felt the sensation within her womb.

His hardness cradled against her belly, she reached to trace a fingertip up and down his shaft, then clasped and pulled him to her.

He entered her with a moan, and she welcomed the fulfillment, climaxing immediately when he put his hands beneath her to lift her hips and plunge

more deeply than she would have thought possible.
When he found his own release, she joined him a
second time.

The wind picked up outside with an eerie, lone-
some howl as the snow scraped the windows, but
inside there was warmth and need and peace.

Alex awoke with Megan nestled to his side and
a chill pervading the room as the fire died. Each
night they spent together bound them closer; and
if she hadn't mentioned the word love to him yet,
Alex was confident she soon would. He smiled
softly with the memory of their recent lovemaking
and turned his face to kiss the top of her head.
Megan murmured his name in her sleep, and the
hand that lay on his chest curled possessively, tangling in the hair that dusted his skin.

He would never let her go. He had wandered
for years from one assignment to the next, the last
year a constant search for Joanna and then Brian
Daily. He had never felt such peace as he felt with
this woman beside him. It was a feeling he would
fight with everything he had to keep.

Someone wanted them both dead and now it
looked as though that someone had killed Megan's
father. He wondered if that person and the man
involved with Joanna were one and the same. It
would save him a lot of time if that were so.

Alex listened to the snow fight with the wind
and knew a severe storm raged outside. There
would be no investigating until the tumult blew itself out.

He inched away from Megan and began to dress. "Where are you going?" she asked sleepily.

"Shh, go back to sleep. I have to return to the barracks."

"It's snowing. Come back to bed." She lifted her hand in invitation.

Alex took her hand and sat on the edge of the bed. "I don't think you'll be open for business for a few days in this weather. I'll be back later."

"Don't leave." She yanked his hand, and he tumbled forward on top of her. Giggling, she wrapped her arms around his neck.

"The day after tomorrow is Christmas," Alex said as he removed her arms from his neck and slid out of her reach.

"Christmas?" Her voice sounded more awake now. "I forgot."

"Maybe we could spend it together?" Alex ventured.

"Yes." She sat up, and in the dim light Alex admired the naked rise and fall of her breasts and the tumble of red hair over her shoulders. "I'll have a special dinner here for everyone. It'll be wonderful," she said.

"I had something more private in mind."

"No, this will be great." She warmed to the subject. "A feast and presents. I've never had a Christmas dinner. We were always working." She looked up at him, her face shining with anticipation. "You'll come?"

He groaned at the image she presented, naked in front of him, her eyes full of happiness and excitement. Though he had dreamed of an evening together in bed for their celebration, he couldn't disappoint her. Swallowing his own disappointment, he said, "I wouldn't miss it."

SIXTEEN

The snow continued throughout the night and the next day. Though Megan didn't lock the doors of The Celebration against customers, no one ventured in, so she and the girls ended up playing cards amongst themselves.

She had debated for the past two days on what to give Alex and had found nothing suitable, even in the town that had everything. When she returned to her room to wrap the presents she had bought, her eyes fell on the sweater she had knitted for Brian during the long months she had been stranded in St. Michael the previous winter. The blue of the yarn reminded her of Alex's eyes and she put her cheek to the wool. She had found his gift.

Christmas day arrived, dark and still snowing. The Celebration was filled with the tantalizing smells of holiday baking. Megan awoke early and lay in her bed enjoying the anticipation of the day.

Papa had always insisted a holiday was a day like any other, only there was more money to be made off the poor saps who believed the day was special.

Somehow, Megan had never been able to convince herself of her father's beliefs in that respect. As each holiday came and went, celebrated by everyone but the Dailys, the emptiness inside Megan had increased. Today she would fill some of that emptiness with the joy of the season.

She dressed for the occasion in the white dress she had worn for her debut as Meggie O'Day. The outfit was her best, and she hadn't worn it since that night. She had told all the dancers to dress for dinner.

Megan crept downstairs as quietly as she could, though she knew everyone else was still asleep, and placed the wrapped packages around the long table set up in the dance hall.

"Merry Christmas, Megan," Alex said.

Megan gasped. She hadn't heard him enter. "How long have you been watching me?"

"Not nearly long enough. You look beautiful, though a bit cold. Here." He stepped toward her, handing her a large box tied with red ribbon. "You might prefer this."

"For me?" she asked, a pleased smile tugging at the edges of her lips.

"Who else? Open it."

Megan stared down at the box in her hands, savoring the moment. She hadn't had a present since her mother died. Slowly she slid the ribbon from the box and pulled off the lid. Inside lay folds of green velvet of a shade she knew would flatter her skin and hair to their utmost. She pulled the dress from the box and held it up to her chest.

The style was one she would have favored before coming to the Yukon, plain and high necked, boasting leg-of-mutton sleeves and a full skirt. A ruffled flounce was sewn around the hem.

Her eyes met Alex's and she smiled. "Thank you. It's lovely."

"Would you wear it today?" He moved so close, the heat of his body called to hers. "Wear it for me."

"I'll change now." Megan moved to the stairs and began to climb. She paused when she realized Alex wasn't following.

"Ah . . . wouldn't you like to come up?" She blushed at how brazen the words sounded, then chided herself for her silliness. The man had slept in her bed and she was embarrassed to ask him to her room.

"I'll just wait here," Alex said. "I'd like to see you walk down the stairs in that dress. Just for me."

Megan found that image arousing, and she wet her lips with her tongue. When she glanced at Alex's face, his attention had focused on her mouth. The bared skin of her shoulders and neck warmed with the thought of what his lips were capable of doing to her.

She stepped forward, but Alex stepped back, putting a hand up between them. "If I kiss you now, Megan, I'll take you upstairs and we won't leave your room again today. I know how much you've looked forward to this dinner. We'll save our time for later."

Megan nodded, touched that he understood her

need for the trappings of a holiday. After allowing herself one small touch of a finger to his lips, she left him alone in the dance hall.

Alex admired the sway of her hips in the white satin dress. He remembered the first time he'd seen her in that dress, how he'd despised her and everything she stood for. He was ashamed to admit he had been such a prig. He had no conception of what a woman alone had to endure, but Megan had taught him much about true strength and courage.

A door opened upstairs and Alex jumped in surprise. She couldn't be dressed already. Perhaps she needed help with a fastening. Alex moved to the stairs and glanced up, then immediately ducked behind the stairwell out of sight.

It was not Megan who had exited from her room but Queen, her dark, hooded cape swaying as she crept stealthily down the hall. Alex was lawman enough to recognize the behavior of a woman with something to hide.

He remained under the stairs, praying Megan would not return at that inopportune moment. When he heard the back door close behind Queen, he emerged from the shadows. Torn, he glanced upstairs and then at the closed door.

No time to tell Megan what had happened. If he wanted to know what Queen was up to, he had to follow her now or lose her in the storm.

Alex picked up his coat and followed Queen out the door.

* * *

Megan stood in front of the floor-length mirror, admiring her gift. The dress fit as if it had been made for her, and most likely it had. She had pulled her hair into a loose roll at her neck, the more elaborate style she had fashioned for the white dress seeming out of place with the simpler green velvet. She cocked her head and the mirror image of Megan cocked her head, as well. She liked this dress better, if the truth be told. Alex would, too.

She went to the door and took a deep breath, suddenly nervous, though she didn't know why. Yanking open the door, she told Damon to stay, though he eagerly pushed at her legs in an attempt to get past. She glanced down and saw a shadowed figure at the back of the hall.

"I'm ready," she called and began her descent.

As she walked down the stairs, Megan attempted to gauge Alex's reaction, but he stubbornly remained in the dark where she could see nothing but a vague outline. When she reached the floor she stopped and did a slow turn so he could see the full glory of the gift. His continued silence unnerved her, and she walked across the floor, squinting into the dark corner of the room where he leaned against the wall.

"Well, what do you think?" she demanded.

The figure straightened and moved into the light.

"You!" she gasped before a hand clamped over her lips.

* * *

Alex followed the cloaked figure through the snow, staying back far enough to remain undetected but staying close enough not to lose his quarry in the swirling, stinging whiteness. Queen was headed for Paradise Alley. Amazement flooded him when she knocked on the door to Geraldine's cottage and was admitted without question.

He hesitated at the door, wondering if the two women were acquainted, though his friend had never mentioned knowing Queen. Perhaps they were merely sharing the Christmas morning together. Well, if that were the case, no harm in his joining them.

Geraldine took an inordinate amount of time to answer his knock, and the surprise on her face had Alex pushing his way into the cottage without her leave.

"Where is she?" His gaze swept the empty cottage, taking in the snoring pup on the bed.

"Who?"

"Queen Love I followed her from The Celebration."

"Ah . . . she . . . um . . . left," Geraldine stammered.

Alex wrenched open the rear door, striding back into the storm. His eyes strained against the snow, but he caught no glimpse of the cloaked figure. With a sigh, he returned to the cottage, confident he could question Queen later after he had done the same with Geraldine.

"Why was she here?" Alex asked.

"She brought me some things." Geraldine indicated the food on the table with a nervous gesture.

"You never mentioned you were friends."

Geraldine wandered about the room, her shoulders tense and her eyes averted. "No? It must have slipped my mind."

"What's wrong, Geraldine?" Alex crossed the room and took her hands in his, forcing the woman to look into his face. Her gaze slipped from his, and he put his hands on her shoulders. "Tell me what you're hiding."

He followed her nervous gaze to a chair near the window. He strode across the room and lifted Ian McMurphy's fur coat into the air.

"You've been hiding Ian?" he said incredulously, betrayal a bitter taste at the back of his throat. "All this time you knew I was looking for him. He's suspected of trying to kill me, Geraldine. Were you a part of that, too?"

"No! I didn't know. I swear."

She backed away as Alex advanced. "I trusted you. Did you run to him and tell him everything I confided in you?"

Geraldine didn't answer, but her eyes told the truth and Alex turned away with a sound of disgust.

"Why?" he whispered.

"He owns this house, the whole alley. Me. I had to live, baby. You of all people should understand that."

"Where is he now?"

"I don't know. He said he had something to do, that he wouldn't be back till it was done."

"And what does Queen have to do with this?"

"I don't know. She brings food and clothes for us; but she never speaks to me and he tells me nothing."

"Is he behind the attempt on my life and Megan's?"

"Maybe. He wants her father's mine. I don't know why. And he hates you, Alex. It amused him to hide here when he knew all you had done for me."

Alex turned away from the entreaty in Geraldine's eyes. He understood her dilemma, but at the moment the wound was too fresh for forgiveness. Without another word, he opened the door and walked into the cold night.

Inside The Celebration Alex shouted for Queen. When the dancer didn't appear, he ascended the stairs and threw open the door to her room. *Empty.*

"Here, here, Lieutenant. What are ya doin'?" Zechariah asked

"I have to talk to Queen."

"Ain't she there?"

"No," Alex said with a frown. Something was not right here.

"Odd. She should be."

Alex strode down the hall and knocked on Megan's door. When no one answered, he opened it and was nearly knocked down when Damon ran past him and down the stairs to stand whining and clawing at the front door.

"Where's Megan?" Alex asked the old man.

"You're havin' a mighty hard time keepin' track of the women around here, aren't ya, Lieutenant? I ain't seen her this mornin' neither."

Ignoring the man, Alex walked into Megan's room, his gaze taking note of the white dress on the bed and the absence of the green dress he had given her earlier. She had obviously changed as he'd asked and come downstairs to show off the dress. But where had she gone when she found him absent? Certainly not out in the storm.

Alex walked slowly downstairs, Zechariah at his heels. He stared at Damon, who continued to scratch at the door. Absently he opened the door to let the wolf out. Instead of running into the snow, the animal looked at him and waited.

"Looks like he wants you to follow him."

Alex's gaze swept the empty dance hall. Nothing seemed amiss until he noted a gleaming object in the center. Crossing the room, he bent and picked up the sparkling glass necklace Megan had worn the night she became Meggie. The clasp was broken, as if torn from her throat. His hand clenched, making the stones cut into his palm.

Alex took in the anxious wolf who awaited him at the door. Ian was missing and so was Queen. Now he couldn't find Megan, and her wolf was very determined to lead him somewhere. If he didn't miss his guess, he would find at least one, or all three, of the missing residents of Dawson City at the end of the wolf's trail.

"Well, Damon, looks like it's you and me to the

rescue this time." He pulled his hat down over his ears and turned his collar about his neck before following the black wolf into the storm.

He stopped at the mounted police headquarters only long enough to order a search party to follow him. The snow was slowing down, and he had no doubt they would be able to follow his tracks. He declined to wait, knowing the tracks of Megan's kidnapper had already been obliterated. He would have to depend on the tracking abilities of Damon to find her; and the sooner the wolf was on the trail, the better.

Alex retrieved his horse and Damon set off, nose to an invisible trail. They went slowly, struggling through the deep drifts. At first the horse shied from the scent of wolf; but after a half hour, when the wolf acted more like a dog and paid no attention to the horse, the animal settled in.

Alex's extremities soon went numb with cold. That didn't matter. It didn't take him long to see where they were headed. He had passed upon the same path before, under the same conditions.

He smelled the smoke from the cabin's fire and knew he had been correct in his assumption. At the rise behind the cabin, he called the wolf back. He did not know what, or who, awaited him below. With a firm command, he ordered Damon to remain on the hill.

Cautiously he crept to the rear door, knowing the wind muffled any sound of his approach. If he were lucky, Megan would be inside and unhurt and the kidnapper would not expect anyone to arrive in the storm.

Pulling his revolver, Alex checked the weapon, then took a deep breath and kicked open the door. He crouched low, ready to fire at the slightest movement.

"Who's there?" Megan cried.

"Are you alone?"

An audible sigh of relief drifted on the smoke-scented air. Megan's sigh. "Yes. But I don't know for how long. Get me out of here."

Alex crossed the room, gaze darting into every corner. He reached the bed and anger filled him at the sight of her tied hand and foot. He dropped to his knees by the bed, setting the revolver on the floor nearby before releasing Megan.

As soon as she was free, she launched herself into his arms and he held her tightly, not realizing until that moment how frightened he had been since he had discovered her missing. His lips descended upon hers, desperate to prove to himself that she was well and safe in his arms.

Megan kissed him back just as desperately, her hands pushing his hat from his head to tangle in his hair and pull him closer. He had been so cold, but within moments his body warmed. Impatiently he yanked off his gloves and cradled the warm, smooth flesh of her cheeks in his hands as he deepened their kiss. When she tried to draw him back with her onto the bed, Alex broke the embrace with a groan. Now was not the time for such a reunion, though his body might demand one.

Instead, Alex sat on the bed, drawing Megan onto his lap, where her head fell naturally into the crook of his shoulder.

"How did you find me?" she asked.

"Damon. Who brought you here?"

"Ian.

He should have known. "Ian's been hiding at Geraldine's all this time. And Queen is missing. Have you seen her?"

"No."

"That doesn't mean she isn't around somewhere."

"What possible reason would Queen have for kidnapping me?"

"I intend to find that out." Alex put her on her feet and stood. "But first I want to get you back to town. There should be a search party not too far behind me." He yanked the fur rug from the bed and put it around her. "Are you up to the trip?"

"I'll follow you anywhere," she said with a smile.

"That's my girl. Let's go." He was reaching for his revolver when the door swung open.

"Carson, leave the gun right where it is and step away from Meggie. Nice and slow."

SEVENTEEN

"McMurphy, I've been looking for you." Alex stepped away from Megan, his gaze on the rifle in Ian's hands.

"I know. Slide that revolver right on over here and then go sit against the wall." Ian motioned with the gun.

Alex complied, cursing himself for being caught in such a situation. But he had bested Ian in a fight before and he could do so again. If he could only get rid of the guns.

"What's the meaning of this, McMurphy?" Megan demanded.

Ignoring her question, Ian crossed the room and shoved her back on the bed. Alex stood up, but when Ian cocked the revolver and leveled it at him, he subsided. The big man quickly retied Megan, then pulled a chair over and as efficiently tied Alex into it. "That should hold you two until Willie comes," Ian remarked.

"Willie? You know Willie?" Megan exclaimed.

"Of course I know my partner."

A sound from the door made Ian frown and he

stalked over to glance outside. A bundle of snarling black fur hit him in the chest, and he staggered but did not fall. The wolf hit the floor and came up on all fours, crouched for another leap. Megan and Alex watched in helpless horror as Ian raised his rifle.

"No!" Megan screamed.

But before Ian could fire the gun, Damon leapt, his teeth sinking into Ian's free hand. The big man howled in pain, then brought the rifle across to smash the butt against Damon's skull. The wolf released his hold and crumpled to the floor.

"I'll kill you for that, McMurphy." Tears welled in Megan's eyes.

"I don't think you'll have the opportunity. Not before you die, anyway." Ian dragged the wolf's limp body outside. He returned to wait just inside the open door.

"So, what's your plan?" Alex asked.

"I'm not the planner in this partnership; that's Willie."

"Where's Queen?" Megan asked.

Ian raised his eyebrows. "Oh, she's around."

"With Willie?"

Ian laughed. "Yeah, she's with Willie. They'll be here soon." He looked at Alex. "Didn't expect to find you here though. I've wanted to take care of you all along, but Willie said no. Now there won't be any choice. Suits me just fine. I knew you were trouble as soon as I heard your name."

"You knew Joanna?" Alex ventured.

"Knew her." Ian snorted. "You could say that. Brought her here from San Francisco."

"What about Brian?"

"They were friends. He tried to warn her against me, but she wouldn't listen. Even when we got here, he gave her a job, hopin' she'd leave me be. But I could always promise her more than Brian could."

"Because you lied and Papa wouldn't," Megan muttered.

Ian grinned, shrugged. "Part of my charm. Josie was good company till she got pregnant; then she got whiny. Always talkin' about the kid, how I had to do right by her."

"So you left her on Paradise Alley." Alex's fury grew, increased by the knowledge that he couldn't get his hands around the man's throat.

"Of course. Perfect place for her. How was I to know she was so weak? Women have kids all the time. They don't go and kill themselves over it."

"You're disgusting," Megan said from the bed.

"I'd watch my mouth if I were you, Meggie. I've always had a taste for redheads."

"You won't touch her," Alex stated.

"And what do you plan to do about it, Carson?"

"I'll kill you slowly, instead of quickly as I'd planned."

Ian laughed, loud and long, slapping his thighs for emphasis. "Can't wait to see you try. I haven't had such a good laugh since old Brian tried to fight me before I killed him."

"You killed my father?" Megan said softly.

"Of course. Willie said he was gettin' too close to the gold."

"What gold?" Alex asked, trying to keep Ian's attention away from Megan.

"The gold on this claim." Ian looked at him as if he were a half-wit. "You don't know anything do you? Willie and Brian were partners. Willie hired me to do the mining on this claim. We found gold and then decided to get rid of Brian so we could have the gold ourselves. Brian made it easy, going off on a trip the way he did after I sent him that note. Easy enough to set off an avalanche on that pass, and then no one even went lookin' for him. Thought I killed that damn wolf, too. Should have shot it." He glanced out the door. "Hell and damnation, he's gone." Without another word, Ian went in search of Damon.

Megan turned to look at Alex. "I can't believe he murdered my father, and all those innocent people on the pass. Papa was so gentle and kind. He loved adventures and new ideas." She sighed and closed her eyes. "I feel like I've lost him all over again."

The red rage inside Alex hardened into a cold knot of fury. "I know what you mean."

Immediately her eyes flew open, her gaze searching out his. "I'm sorry. To hear about your sister that way. From that . . . that . . . brute." She jerked on the bonds with a futile gesture. "I want to scratch his eyes out."

"I had something a little more painful in mind."

"We've got to get out of here before Ian comes

back. You heard what he said. When Willie and Queen get here, they're going to kill us." Megan bit her lip. "I can't believe Queen is involved in this. She was my friend. I trusted her, confided in her, and all along she was after my father's gold."

"I'll take care of her, too."

"Not if you're bound hand and foot like a Christmas goose," Megan pointed out.

"But I'm not bound hand and *foot,* and that's where Ian made his first mistake."

"What?"

Alex lifted his boot onto the bed near Megan's bound hands. "I've got a knife in my boot. If you can just get it out, we'll be free in no time."

Megan looked at him with admiration. *"Preparation* really is your middle name, isn't it?"

"I do my best."

Megan twisted onto her side to give her fingers better access to his boot, and Alex leaned back, trying to think of a way to get them both out of the cabin alive.

Megan's fingers were sore and her head ached, but she almost had the knife worked to the top of Alex's boot. Then would come the task of releasing Alex's hands. He had been surprisingly patient and gentle with her fumbling attempts to rescue the knife. She could tell by the still, cold set of his face he was planning their escape—and Ian's demise.

Her fingers closed around the handle of the knife and she was able to draw it slowly from the boot. Her eyes met Alex's and he smiled. Then his gaze went to the door as the sound of barking dogs approached.

Within minutes the sound came closer stopping before the cabin. Shortly thereafter the door slammed open, and Megan pushed the knife back into Alex's boot.

Startled, she looked up to encounter a tall, broad figure in a hooded bearskin coat. She could make out no features beneath the shadow of the hood as the being's head swung to and fro, scanning the cabin. The long, mournful howl of a wolf rent the night, and the figure whirled, returning outside without a word.

Megan released a sigh that turned into a groan when Alex replaced his boot next to her hands. She would have to start all over again in her attempt to retrieve the knife.

This time she was able to retrieve the knife more quickly. Her hands shook with tension as she tried to steady the blade. If only they had enough time to get free.

As if in denial to her wish, the door swung open again, re-admitting Ian and the figure swathed in bearskin. Megan slipped the knife under her pillow.

"I can't help it, Willie," Ian was saying as they entered. "I thought the cursed animal was dead. If he comes back I'll shoot 'im this time."

The cloaked figure said nothing, and from Ian's nervous shuffling of feet, that was a bad sign. Megan kept her eyes on the figure, wondering what Willie had done to make Ian's bullying demeanor shift so abruptly.

"Well, you two have been wondering about Willie, so here you go. Made a right big nuisance of yourself about it, too. Too bad you won't live to tell anyone our little secret."

"Where's Queen?" Megan asked. Had the two done away with her, as well?

"Right here, Lovey."

Megan's mouth fell open in surprise as the coat fell to the floor to reveal the immense dancer. "I—I—don't understand," Megan stammered.

"Of course you don't. You're not supposed to," Queen soothed.

"Enough of this," Alex said. "Where's Willie Shore?"

"Right here, Lieutenant." Queen threw back her head and cackled. "Willie's me and I'm Willie."

"You're Willie Shore?" Megan asked. "But how?"

"Everyone has an alias in Dawson City, and I'm no exception. I was born Wilhemina Shore. I came up to the Yukon to get away from a little trouble I had in California. No one here but your Papa knew me as anyone but Queen Love."

"How could you kill him, Queen?" Megan found herself unable to call the woman by any other name.

Queen looked at her, confused. "I didn't kill him. Ian did."

"And you didn't know about it?" Alex asked.

"I didn't say that. I'm just saying I didn't kill

him. Ian was getting jealous of how fond I was of Brian, and there was the gold and all. One night I said, 'Well, if you hate him so much, why don't you get rid of him.' The next thing I knew, Brian was dead.'' She shrugged and sat at the table.

Megan couldn't believe the woman could sit and calmly talk about Brian's death. She wanted to break something into tiny pieces, preferably Queen's face.

"You've been lying to me all along," Megan said.

"True. But it had to be done. I never expected you to show up in the Yukon. Then when you did and refused to leave, I thought maybe if I made The Celebration a success you wouldn't bother with the claim. Hadn't figured the lieutenant would help you out." Queen frowned at Alex.

"Did you know my sister?" Alex asked.

"Sure did. Pretty little thing. But once Ian and I were partners, she had to go. Never thought she'd fall apart that way, though."

Megan could tell by the set of Alex's jaw that he was having as hard a time as she dealing with Queen's casual attitude toward death and murder. The woman believed any means justified the end as long as she got what she desired.

"So, when we started to get too close to the answers, you tried to kill us?" Alex prompted.

"That was my idea," Ian said as he lounged in the doorway. "I put black snakeroot in your punch and had one of the miners give it to you. Too bad you only took a swallow."

"Yes, too bad," Alex muttered.

"Then," Ian continued, "when that didn't work, I took a shot at Meggie here. I could tell you were real sweet on her, and I figured if she were gone you wouldn't keep sniffin' around. But I ain't too good of a shot."

"Ain't that the truth." Queen narrowed her gaze upon Ian.

Megan realized then that Queen merely tolerated Ian, taking advantage of his strength and his feelings for her. Everyone in Dawson City had thought Ian a man with the Midas touch. Now Megan witnessed the brains behind his success.

"I wish you had left when you could, Lovey. I grew right fond of you. But now I've got no choice. You and the lieutenant here will have to meet your maker. We'll make it look like an accident so no one starts lookin' for us. Once you're gone, it'll be a small matter to take over The Celebration, and the entire mine will belong to me."

"How do you plan to do this deed?" Alex asked.

Megan threw him an irritated look. He acted as though they were discussing the weather over a cup of tea, rather than their murders while they were tied to the furniture.

"The cabin will burn with you both inside. Happens all the time in these parts. One spark on a fur, and the place goes up in flames while the occupants sleep. Everyone in town knows you two have been keeping to the same bed. No one will be suspicious that you died in the cabin together. It's kind of romantic in a way."

Megan opened her mouth to say a party of

Mounties was on the way, but snapped it shut at a look from Alex.

"Is there a lot of gold on this claim?" Megan asked to buy time.

"Loads, Lovey, loads. This is one of the best stretches of land on the river. Your Pa got it in a card game, but you know how he was about gold claims. He asked me to register it and see about gettin' someone to do the work. We'd be partners. I never thought anything would come of it. One of the few times I was wrong."

Queen heaved herself to her feet, walked over to the bed, and looked down at Megan. Megan tried not to flinch when Queen touched her face. "I really did like you," she said, as though to herself, then shrugged. "But that's neither here nor there. Bye, Lovey. Have a nice hereafter."

With a nod to Ian, Queen picked up her coat and left without a backward glance.

"What a sweetheart," Alex muttered.

"Don't be sayin' nothin' about my Willie." Ian glared. "She's too smart for the likes of you."

Alex raised his eyebrows and remained silent. Ian looked as though he wanted to take his fists to Alex, and Megan had begun to fear he would give in to the impulse when an impatient call from Queen had Ian swinging away and lumbering to the fireplace. Within seconds, he had set fire to the fur rug and some blankets. He smiled in their direction, bowed, and closed the door. The sound of the dogs retreating soon faded as the crackle of the fire intensified.

"Since no one seems very eager to come to our rescue, I guess we'd better set about taking care of ourselves," Alex observed.

"Do you think someone will arrive soon?" Megan eyed the spreading fire.

"We can't depend on that. Get the knife, Megan; don't look at the fire."

Megan hurriedly complied and set to work on Alex's bonds. Her hands shook at the thought of what could happen if her fingers cramped and refused to function or what would happen if she dropped the knife. The smoke billowed and her eyes burned. Whenever either one of them tried to speak, their words dissolved into a fit of coughing.

Finally, when the smoke was so thick she could no longer see Alex next to her and the fire had come so close the heat was near to unbearable, the rope gave way. Quickly Alex turned the knife on her bonds and helped her to her feet.

Together they ran to the door and Alex pushed. It did not budge. Megan fought the panic swelling within her and the burning sensation in her lungs. How had the fire spread so fast? How had the smoke gotten so thick, so acrid? How could she die this way when she'd finally found the true reason for living? Megan tried to gather another breath, but lost the battle and fell into the swirling, gray mist where she knew no more.

Alex pushed against the door. Megan collapsed to the floor beside him. He had to get her out or he would lose her.

He shoved the door again, panic lending him strength. This time it moved. Again he pushed. Again the door shifted. Gathering his remaining strength, Alex backed up and ran full force at the door, turning at the last second to slam his shoulder against the portal.

The door burst open. He fell into the snow, dazed, breathing the painfully fresh air in loud gulps. Stumbling to his feet, he returned to the inferno and dragged Megan outside.

She lay so still, his heart nearly stopped. But when he put his ear to her chest, a faint whisper of breath touched his cheek. She still lived. His own breathing resumed.

Lightly he slapped her cheeks. "Megan. Come on, love; don't do this to me now."

A noise made him glance up, then rise swiftly to his feet as several Mounties with a dog sled and team came over the rise, Damon running in the lead. The wolf ran directly to Megan and licked her face. At her lack of response he pawed her shoulder gently, then sat back on his haunches to glare at Alex.

"I didn't do anything," Alex said, wondering why he felt compelled to defend himself to an animal.

"What the hell is going on here, Carson?"

Alex ignored his fellow Mountie and knelt again at Megan's side. She seemed to be breathing easier and her color had improved. He kissed her forehead and smoothed her hair, his eyes intent on her face until she moaned his name softly and began to stir. Then he got to his feet. Now that help had arrived and she was safe, he had business to take care of.

After speaking briefly to the leader of the search party, Alex took the reins of the team and, cracking the whip over the dogs' heads, pursued Ian and Queen.

They had a good start, but their trail was fresh and easy to follow. Alex hoped that the lighter weight of his sled would allow him to overcome them.

His anger had burned while he listened to the cold-blooded way Queen spoke of the deaths of Brian and Joanna. The fact that he was bound and unable to retaliate had made his fury increase tenfold. He ached to get his hands on Ian, the murderer, and Queen, the mastermind. They would not soon forget what pain felt like.

He glimpsed a movement ahead and urged the dogs to a faster pace. Soon, he pulled from a copse of trees and saw his quarry before him. Ian whipped up his team, but the dogs were too winded and Alex gained inch by icy inch upon them.

Queen fired a shot, but the momentum of the sled threw off her aim and the bullet flew harmlessly into the sky. She shouted to Ian, and they switched places, Queen driving the team and Ian taking possession of the gun.

Alex was directly behind their sled and snow flew up into his eyes, nearly blinding him. When his vision cleared, he saw Queen shove Ian from the sled. The big man fell into the path of Alex's dogs and Alex's sled overturned, tossing him onto the hard ground along with his enemy. Queen continued, never glancing back to see what had become of her partner.

Before Alex could get to his feet, McMurphy sent him sprawling onto the ground; his mouth filled with snow and ice. Luckily, the fall had dislodged Ian's gun. Their fates would be decided on the virtue of their fists and wits alone.

Alex was able to shove McMurphy off his back and they both struggled to their feet.

"I've been waiting for this a long time, Carson." McMurphy smiled.

"I owe you, Ian." Alex punctuated his words with a right strike to the man's jaw. "And I intend to give you your due."

They circled each other, like two bears meeting for the first time. Ian dove for Alex's knees, and they both went down on the snow-covered ground. They rolled over and over; and when they came to a stop, Ian straddled Alex's chest. Alex lurched sideways to avoid a punch from Ian's ham-like fist.

"Your sister was the worst girl I ever had. Knew nothin' about how to please a man. But I taught her well."

Ian was breathing heavily, but he aimed another punch at Alex's face. This one glanced off Alex's temple, and the world rocked. The sky above came back into focus along with another fist barreling toward his face, and Alex shoved Ian with all his might. The unexpected movement sent the man careening to the ground, allowing Alex to gain his feet.

"Once I was through teachin' her—" Ian climbed to his feet. "—Joanna was the best whore in town."

With a roar of rage, Alex ducked his head and barreled into Ian's chest. The force of his attack propelled them both backward. The ground gave way beneath them, and they fell through the air. Down, down, down . . .

EIGHTEEN

Megan groaned and tried to lift her body away from the pressing dampness she lay upon. Something warm and wet bathed her face, and her eyes snapped open.

"Damon." She hugged the wolf to her, tried to sit up, and fell back, coughing.

"Here now, miss, you don't have to sit up. Just rest a spell," a strange voice soothed as gentle hands pushed her back.

Megan squinted against the darkness, illuminated slightly from the flames of the cabin, and saw she was surrounded by Mounties. The sight of the men reminded her of the search party Alex had mentioned earlier.

At the thought of Alex, she struggled to a sitting position, her gaze seeking his face among those around her. When she didn't find him, she scanned the ground around her, but saw no one else.

"Where's Alex?" she demanded of the Mountie who had spoken to her.

Fear clawed at her. The last thing she remembered was a burning cabin. Had she gotten out somehow while he had perished?

Her gaze rested fearfully on the still-burning structure and the Mountie hastened to assure her. "The lieutenant took off after McMurphy on the dog sled."

Megan slumped with relief, and Damon took the opportunity to bathe her face again. The action made her aware of just how damp she had become lying in the snow, and she forced herself to stand. Another coughing bout rewarded her efforts, but she waved away the offers of assistance and remained on her feet.

"You'd best go after him."

"Sorry, miss. He ordered us to say with you."

Just then a gunshot echoed in the crisp cold air and everyone went still. She stared transfixed at the line of trees into which the dog sled trail disappeared.

"If you *men* won't go after him," she said through clenched teeth, "then I will. Come on, Damon."

Megan hurried along the trail with the wolf at her heels. When she glanced back, a line of red coats streamed in her wake.

Alex and Ian hit the ground with enough force to drive the breath from both their lungs. Alex recovered first and took in their surroundings. He and Ian had fallen over a cliff hidden from view by the thick snow. Luckily they had landed on a small piece of ground jutting out from the cliff's side.

Alex looked up and saw they had fallen about twenty feet. When he looked over the ledge, he swallowed; there were about two hundred feet left to fall and a lake of ice to meet the unlucky.

Ian groaned, then shifted, and Alex sat up, wary of the big man's next move.

"What happened?" Ian mumbled.

"We fell over the edge." Alex pointed up. "A few more feet out and we would both be dead."

Ian glanced over the edge and grimaced, then stood, craning his neck back and gazing at the ice-covered rock face in front of him.

"How the hell we gonna get up that?" he asked.

"There's a party of Mounties at the cabin. They should be along any time now."

Alex watched Ian for any sudden moves. The man had wanted to kill him moments before. Alex wouldn't put it past Ian to shove him over the edge as an afterthought.

"I'm afraid, boys, I can't let you be rescued."

Alex looked up to see Queen, leaning over the cliff to stare at them.

"Honey, throw down a rope," Ian said, relief evident in his voice. "We can leave the lieutenant here and make our escape."

"I'm afraid that won't work for me, Ian. I just came back to make sure you were dead. Now that I see you're not, I'll have to take care of that little detail myself."

Ian frowned in confusion. "What're you talkin' about?"

"Now that you got me the gold, I don't need you anymore; and since I can't have you comin' after me whinin' for your half, I'll have to get rid of you." She swung her gaze to Alex. "And since you'll be unlucky enough to see the dirty deed, you'll have to die, too." A pistol appeared in Queen's hand. Before Alex could say anything to dissuade her, she cocked the gun and shot Ian in the chest.

Alex reached for the man, but Ian was too close to the ledge. He tumbled backward, falling into oblivion at an ever-increasing rate. Alex closed his eyes against the sight of Ian hitting the ice-packed earth, but the sound of McMurphy's scream echoed in the cold air.

The sound of a gun being cocked cracked across the icy air, and Alex turned to meet his fate.

Megan broke through the trees with Damon and the Mounties right behind. Ahead, someone lay in the snow and her heart leapt in fear. But the body did not wear the scarlet coat of the mounted police. Rather, it was covered in bearskin.

"Queen!"

The figure's head jerked, and the hood fell back, exposing Queen's counterfeit blond hair. When the woman got to her feet, Megan's gaze was riveted to the pistol in her hand.

"Alex!" Megan tried to run faster. But the exertion on her already overworked lungs was too much and she fell to the cold ground, coughing and gasping as the Mounties and the wolf surged past her.

Queen sprinted to the nearby dog sled and cracked her whip above the heads of the animals. The team lurched into motion, pulling away from the Mounties at an increasing rate. Another team tugged at their tangled harnesses a few yards in front of Queen and several of the pursuing officers untangled the lines and continued after her.

Megan called Damon back and with his help was able to struggle onward to meet the few Mounties who had remained behind.

"Alex," she gasped to the first man.

The officer pointed to the area where Queen had been lying when they came upon her, and Megan stumbled toward it.

"Hold on, miss; that's a cliff there. Wouldn't want you to tumble on down with the lieutenant."

At the Mountie's words, Megan jerked her elbow from the man's startled grasp and hurried to the edge of the precipice. Fear clenched her throat at the thought of viewing Alex's broken body on the ground below, but she bit her lip and made herself look over the edge.

"Hello," Alex said and Megan jumped back with a squeak of surprise.

She leaned over once again, and Alex waved to her from a ledge below. Megan let out the breath she had been holding. "I thought you were dead."

"Not me." He pointed downward.

She followed his finger and saw the body of Ian

McMurphy far below. She raised a questioning eyebrow in Alex's direction.

"I didn't throw him over if that's what you're thinking," Alex assured her.

"Well?" Megan prompted when he didn't elaborate.

"Queen shot him."

"I thought they were partners."

"Evidently her partners have a bad habit of turning up dead. Just like your father."

"Move aside, miss, so we can haul him up."

Megan glanced up to see several Mounties waiting to lower a rope. She stood, brushed the snow from her clothes, and backed away to allow the officers access. In short order the Mounties pulled Alex over the edge. As soon as he was free of the rope, she fell into his arms.

"When I woke up and you weren't there I was so afraid," Megan whispered against his lips.

"I knew you'd be safe with the men and Damon." He kissed her forehead. "I'm sorry I frightened you."

Megan pulled back and looked into his eyes. As she gazed into their cool, blue depths she knew she loved him. She had fought the emotion, telling herself she didn't need a man in her life, didn't need to endure the inevitable pain he would bring her. But the only pain she could not endure would be the pain of living her life without Alex Carson. They had come so close to losing each other, losing any chance of a life together, she had to take what-